FRONT LINES: COURAGE

Without a Parachute

Sonderho Press, Prescott, ON K0E 1T0

Published 2022.

Edited by Jesse Cohoon, Maria Ford, Thomas Gannon Hamilton.

Printed in Canada on acid-free paper.

ISBN: 978-1-7774267-5-0

Cover art: The Window. Nicole Little

This is the procrastination of a window. That's real painter's tape, laid down haphazardly. Those shadows are unreal and indulgent. But maybe there is enough window on this cover to glimpse the one you hold in your mind.

So, too, it is with the stories within these pages. Stories, like pictures, need an audience. These authors have drawn you frames and panes and views, but you must interpret to understand, and you will always add your influence as you read. It becomes your view, no matter who constructed the window. So, have a generous heart when you open the pages of this book. You are its hidden editor, changing meaning by reflection.

Nicole Little is a visual artist. She is just as meta in real life as you would expect.
littleneocreative.com

FRONT LINES: COURAGE

Without a Parachute

Editors:
Jesse Cohoon,
Maria Ford,
Thomas Gannon Hamilton

SONDERHO PRESS

Foreword

ROLAND GULLIVER

As human beings, we place many assumptions and allusions upon ourselves and the world around us. We are often quick to judge so much on face value. We are often quick to dismiss our own creative abilities, placing the literary and the "Author" on a pedestal breathing the rarified air beyond our knowing.

But we all have stories, we all have experiences, that make, shape, and break us. We are palimpsest: layers upon layers of stories, some erased, some visible. What differentiates us is that not all of us have the tools or the craft to express those stories, to understand those experiences. Importantly, and often overlooked, these tools can be given, shared, explained, trained, and honed to enable anyone to tell their story.

The construction and shaping of a narrative begin to give meaning to our thoughts and actions; finding a structure to what happens, what we think, or what we imagine opens understanding, solace, and joy. Being able to better connect with ourselves and to express that connection can change so many things in our lives.

Many years ago, I stood in the Scottish Parliament at the opening of an exhibition by an organisation called Art in Hospital. One of the artists, a man in his late seventies, talked of his initial reluctance to participate in the art classes turning into a compulsion to paint; he talked about how happy it made him, both when he was painting and in the rest of his day-to-day life. Incredibly, he said, "I now talk to my wife more than I have ever done in the past." Creating is a process of unlocking.

I often wonder why we write. Why is it that writing, and thus reading, is so fundamental to expression and communication? What happens when the thought or idea moves through our brain into our body's action, to be interpreted in words put down on a page, whether it is with a pen, a keyboard, or a voice? And why does seeing or hearing our story externalized change how we comprehend ourselves?

And then there is the simple creative joy of making stories, creating pictures and emotions with words. The strange alchemy of finding the right word. As adults, we adhere to another assumption: that we should surrender our make-believe worlds of childhood for the serious perspective of adulthood. But we are all storytellers, story makers, story sharers, story listeners, and story lovers. Whether that is telling stories to ourselves, our families and friends, or through the printed page.

The art, craft, and community of writing and storytelling is at the heart of what the Writers Collective of Canada (WCC) does. WCC gives an invaluable gift. They give people the means and tools to come together to make stories. They create spaces for those needing support. They show why creativity is fundamental to our health and wellbeing. The results are beautifully represented in this publication through the poems, stories, and pictures of those who took part in the 2021/22 Write On! programme.

The work created in this book, and by the programme, captures the importance of being able to tell one's story, the potential we all have, given time, support, safety, and freedom to express ourselves. The quality of the pieces is breathtaking, heartbreaking, uplifting, and inspiring. Like all good stories, they make us pause to look more at the world around us, make us think differently, and they share the magic of making things up.

We always need stories—to tell, hear, and read more stories. We need more organizations like Writers Collective of Canada. The more stories we hear, the more perspectives we contain, the more layers are added to our understanding of the world and who we are, and the more connections we make between teller and listener, writer, and reader.

The more stories we tell, create, and listen to, the more we will cast aside those assumptions and allusions of ourselves and the world around us.

Roland Gulliver
Director
Toronto International Festival of Authors
January 2022

Introduction

Jesse Cohoon

The Writers Collective of Canada (WCC) authors are the bedrock of the Front Lines anthologies. Like the *Little Prince*, they open their hearts to us, seeing worlds that others can only imagine through their poetry, stories, graphics, and memoirs. The Write On! program began as a passion project developed to provide access for community voices traditionally underheard. It has been my privilege and honour to work with these talented writers for the past five years.

> *"And now here is my secret, a very simple secret: It is only with the heart that one can see rightly; what is essential is invisible to the eye."*
>
> Antoine de Saint-Exupéry, *The Little Prince*

I am amazed at how quickly people come together, either onsite in libraries and community spaces, or virtually. They support each other and reveal deep truths and intimacies, some for the first time. Whether they are just beginning their creative journey or have been published, these WCC writers have been heard, and their courage to share their stories is revealed through their powerful words.

Based on the essential practices of the WCC and guided by mentors, first 23, then 34, and now 63 emerging authors share their stories in six *Front Lines* anthologies. The three new anthologies: *Only One Question*, *Without a Parachute*, and *I open my mouth and speak*, reflect themes of Hope, Courage, and Resilience. Each page is a thread creating a rich tapestry of images, emotions, and experiences, revealing our common humanity in all its complexity.

The authors' notes at the end of the anthologies speak volumes. The authors were supported in their journies by mentors who went beyond the requirements and expectations of the program to share their knowledge and they are rewarded for that commitment. The program's first mentors, Puneet Dutt, Bänoo Zan, Pat Connors, Julie Hartley, Susan Ksiezopolski, and Jay Teitel created a foundation that the current group of mentors: O. Stephen Peart, Brittany Chung Campbell, Lisa Richter, Nadja Lubiw-Hazard, Anna Lee-Popham, TG Hamilton, Bernadette Wagner, Jay Teitel, and Shannon Leahy, have built upon. Early on, Sage Tyrtle's dynamic workshops revealed ways to help bring their stories from the page to spoken word events.

Thanks to Toronto Poet Laureate, Al Moritz; WCC Founder, Susan Turk Mozer; Kate Marshall Flaherty; and TG Hamilton, for providing insight into the foundation that shapes the Write On! experience. Roland Gulliver, Director of the Toronto International Festival of Authors, adds his voice in a Foreword to the three 2022 *Front Lines* anthologies, in which he reflects: "The art, craft, and community of writing and storytelling is at the heart of what the Writers Collective of Canada does."

Special thanks to:

- Jay Teitel, who had no idea what he was getting into when I asked him after a hockey game to share his knowledge
- Susan Ksiezopolski and Steve Elliot, for their efforts in creating a new WCC Chapter in Peel region for writers to experience the WCC magic
- Janet Creery, for leading a dynamic and thriving WCC Chapter in Ottawa
- Roland Gulliver and the Toronto International Festival of Authors, who immediately saw the value of the program
- Daniel MacIvor, Jonathan Goldsmith, Laurie-Shawn Borzovoy, and Andrew Burashko, at the Art of Time Ensemble, in partnership with Harbourfront Centre, for providing a concert of voices with thirteen of the authors in spring of 2022 called *Who Is We? Voices Across the Divides*
- TG Hamilton, Susan Ksiezopolski, and Shannon Leahy, whose comments are always insightful and based in kindness

- Siobhan Lant, whose friendship and attention to detail are invaluable to the development and realization of this and so many other WCC initiatives

Artists, editors, and publishers have contributed their talents to enhance the look and feel of the anthologies.

Sue Reynolds and James Dewar of Piquant Press shared their knowledge of how to self-publish with the writers and created the layout and style for the first three anthologies. Todd Coopee, Maria Ford, and Denis Savoie of Sonderho Press have expanded the reach of the program through their dedicated efforts on the new 2022 anthologies.

Front Cover Artists, Naomi Laufer (Black Rose) and TG Hamilton in the first three anthologies; and Nicole Little, who created the cover art for the new anthologies. Their work reflects the kaleidoscope of cultures represented and the stories found between the covers.

The editing teams of the first three anthologies—TG Hamilton, Julie Hartley, Susan Ksiezopolski, Yazan Alhajali, Puneet Dutt, Bänoo Zan, Richard Mozer, and Susan Turk Mozer—devoted hours to the curation of the anthologies to create a style and internal flow. My co-editors, on the three 2022 anthologies, Maria Ford and TG Hamilton, have added layers of thoughtful nuance to the latest editions. Any typos or errors in the final texts, however unintentional, lay at my feet.

I would also like to thank the staff and independent contractors of the Writers Collective of Canada: Siobhan Lant, Shelley Lepp, Maria Ford, Doug Grundman, Susan Ksiezopolski, Carmel Suttor, Janet Creery, Steve Elliot, Aldonna Stremecki, Sapphire Woods, Abigail Sanderson, Courtney Greenberg, Elliott Fienberg, Alexander Sentsisen, Drew Griffin, Mahsa Hadianfard, and the WCC Board, led by Richard Mozer and Susan Turk Mozer, for their encouragement and support of the Write On! program.

This program has received funding and support from the Ontario Trillium Foundation, the Toronto Arts Council, The Ontario Arts Council, the Azrieli Foundation, BMO Nesbitt Burns, the Toronto Public Library, Working for Change, Union Station, and the Toronto International Festival of Authors. Their contributions have encouraged and empowered many emerging authors.

The current editions are supported by the Ontario Arts Council, The Azrieli Foundation, and the Ontario Trillium Foundation. I would also like to acknowledge the many people who have purchased copies of the anthologies, donated money, and a recent private donation that will help to continue the Write On! program in the future. Thank you all!

We have been in a war for over two years—a health care crisis that may change the fundamental concept of society and human interaction. Throughout these difficult times, the WCC and the Write On! program provided safe haven for anyone looking to explore their voice and expand their creative horizons. The intent is simple: all are welcome, no one is left behind, and every voice is honoured. As we emerge from these challenges, I leave it to a dedicated team of writers, mentors, artists, and supporters to continue the work. May those who join you in the future find their voice and share their incredible journeys of discovery with others.

We all see life through different windows. I am inspired by my mother, Anne, who, isolated by circumstance, uses technology to stay connected and find community, as the writers in these anthologies have. As she looks out her window, sitting in a chair, reading the words that pulse from these pages, she is wrapped in a blanket of hope, courage, and resilience. The voices she hears are many, just beyond a hug.

May the readers of the anthologies hear those voices as well, and feel their own hearts quicken to the sound.

> *"The question is not what you look at, but what you see."*
>
> Henry David Thoreau

Contents

Foreword		**iv**
Introduction		**vi**
There Is A Voice	Bänoo Zan	**xiii**
I Will Believe You		**1**
Courage	Diana Sandulescu	2
Red Badge	Chris Kerr	3
On Three	Mairon Bennett	4
Dear Survivor	Manivillie Kanagasabapathy	5
Aftermath	David Gilkes	6
Daring to Claim the Sky	Jacquie Irvine	7
Courage (in the time of COVID)	Kathleen Conibear	8
Fit in	Dela Muhundarajah	10
The Bed	Sharon Roberts	11
The Bridge and The Dam	Rana Khan	13
Courageous Decision	Lorri Bourgeois	14
Strips of Light		**19**
Moses	Faithlyn Allen	20
Words, words, words	Habeeba	22
Soul Search	Diana Sandulescu	23
Faith in Action	Christina Walsh	24
Out of Hibernation	Vanessa Thompson	27
The Accident and the Incident	Roberta Taylor	28
Journey Home	Janet Anne Kennedy	30
Silent Music	Manivillie Kanagasabapathy	32
Out of quicksand	Maria Habanikova	33
From Within Us We Become Us	Shannon Lintott	35
Looking to Grow		**37**
The Attention Seeker	P.M. Jaye	38
My Pen Leaks	Chris Kerr	39
Surfer Silhouette	Irene Reilly	40
Lakeside	Mairon Bennett	46
Swimming Trilogy	Karen Joan Watson	47

The Trail Before Me ... Vanessa Thompson ... 52
Behind Every Weed Is a Beautiful Flower ... Susan Purser ... 53

I Am From Words ... **55**
Frames From my Window ... Maria Tereza Papaleo ... 56
Unrooting ... Areeba Asghar ... 60
Replete ... Ellise Ramos ... 61
Cosmic Rebirth ... Manivillie Kanagasabapathy ... 62
I Am Glad I Did It ... Sharon Roberts ... 63
I am ... Rooth Vimalanathan ... 65
When the Time Comes ... Joan Sunderland ... 66
Warrior Queen ... Diana Sandulescu ... 71

Memory is a Spider ... **73**
Apophasis ... JL Allderdice ... 74
The Cost of Silence ... Faithlyn Allen ... 75
When I Say I Have Not Written in Three Years ... Luxshie Vimaleswaran ... 76
The land of eternal love ... Habeeba ... 78
Dear Money ... Renee Xu ... 80
My Unfathomable Precious ... Hasib Iftekhar ... 83

Captured and Framed ... **89**
Uncertain Steps ... Yasmin Newson ... 90
Not-So-Great Expectations ... Jeff Cottrill ... 91
Harried ... Kristine Kaposy ... 97
Lost and Found ... Diana Sandulescu ... 99
Too much heart to stay ... María Cristina Sabourin-Jovel (Queen María) ... 100
See You Next Tuesday ... Melissa Peters ... 103
The Photo of What Is ... Susan Purser ... 105

Authors' Notes ... **107**

Mentors' Notes ... **115**

Authors' Biographies ... **119**

Mentors' Biographies ... **127**

About the WCC ... **131**

there is a quiet place ... Kristine Kaposy ... **132**

There Is A Voice

BÄNOO ZAN

that sings your song

opens your veins to
blood

There is a voice
who is not you

gives you words
you never had

invites you
to the allegory
of the cave

There is a voice
in whose tales
you are a myth

shatters your pettiness
and makes you whole

There is a voice
that claims you—
abyss and wings and all

There is a voice
that is yours

when you cross
your borders

There is a voice –

Take yourself
out of its way

Let it sing
through you

Let it make you
a song—

There is a voice

The poem was first published in *Gaea Calling: Community, Insight, Influence*. It then appeared in Voices 2018: A Toronto Writers' Co-operative Anthology and was published in the *Poem in Your Pocket for National Poetry Month*, including work by American and Canadian poets and appeared on a postcard. Published here courtesy of the author.

I Will Believe You

Courage as a gateway virtue leads to authentic voice, faith, honesty, and love.

Courage

Diana Sandulescu

When I think of what it means to show courage,
I reflect on the events of my life
To me having courage means to remain your
authentic self despite circumstances

To not let bad experiences and the traumas
of one`s life change your heart:
If you loved and in turn got hurt,
do not be afraid to love again

It is love and kindness that makes this world
a brighter place
Courage is kindness
Courage is forgiveness
Courage is faith
Courage is hope and so much more

Red Badge

Chris Kerr

I have survived
things
that would have killed
most
or at least
their spirit

not courage
fear motivated
me
afraid to die
to stay
if being in place
treading water

fear
the rabbit hunkers
at your
feet
thinking it can't be
seen

maybe
courage is simply
flushing out your
rabbit
into the bush
it's easily
skittish

On Three

Mairon Bennett

Wild-eyed and beautiful, she had mats in her hair.
In her mind, philosophy and blunt trauma
wrestled each other down
Vomit bright with blood
She would weep for days, trails of eyeliner
smudged, sweating in a dirty bed

All I wanted was to hold her
Her thoughts hovered, suspended in glass
Her laugh sent birds exploding from trees

Her story left me frozen
Mouth open. No words.
Cornered in a horse's stall
Held and stroked and broken
Manure and straw
Her light stuttering, then going out with a pop

Stepping to the bridge and glancing down
(urging the white horse into a gallop,
tanned arms holding
strong)

The books couldn't save her
Each turned page a tiny wish
I couldn't save her
Because I couldn't reach her

So as the clouds gathered and the rain came down
I thought of her
In freefall
Cutting through the air
An exquisite unravelling
Skydiving without a parachute

Dear Survivor

Manivillie Kanagasabapathy

Dear Survivor,

I will be the megaphone
amplifying your voice
when society tries to silence you.

I will be your shield from those
whose protection
comes at the cost of your soul.

I will be your shoulder to lean on
when your pain wants nothing more
than to tear you apart.

But most of all –
I will believe you,
when you tell me *Your* story.

I will show up how you need me,
when you call for me
as you navigate the world.

A victim,
yet a survivor.
Hoping you understand,
that neither define you.

Aftermath

David Gilkes

Falling, falling into these wrong things.
Poor decisions, missed occasions, alone.
Swiftly departing yet slowly forgetting.
Hasty judgments leave you needing to atone.

Every misstep like an unseen earthquake.
Each surrender a deeper knife in the back.
Failing yourself seems beyond all redemption.
Losing your truth sends you hurtling offtrack.

In God's name—what madness has happened?
Why falling still so far from the mark?
Cain had better prospects and manners.
Abel slain by this bite, worse than bark.

Where is forgiveness to be found and asserted?
Not in this dead time, nor even this place.
Exposed as another stubborn, slow learner.
Now you know better, yet still the disgrace.

Never too late to retrieve scattered pieces.
Not while a breath still resides in your chest.
Heed the Spirit that the righteous have looked to.
Call on the courage of those who gave their best.

Daring to Claim the Sky

Jacquie Irvine

When I try something new
I am daring to claim the sky.
When I try.

To someone who doesn't know me,
I look like a bird who broke her wing.
But even birds with broken wings survive
And some even thrive.

We can all sing.
We can all dance.
Some of us never take the chance
But those who try and succeed
In their hearts have claimed the sky.

Daring to claim the sky
Is such a wonderful high
Especially if you succeed.
Confidence is all you need.

Dare to claim the sky.
Don't stop to question why
For why becomes a block
And your ability others mock.

Dare to claim the sky.
Dance if you can't fly.
If I am reincarnated
I want to be a bird.

Courage (in the time of COVID)

Kathleen Conibear

In the dark room on a sweat-drenched sofa she lay, watching the flickering light of the television. The scene was as painful as the empty words of the politician. "Patriots" stormed the Capitol in chaotic technicolor, clapping each other on the back, home-made weapons in hand as they "bravely" took over the house of government. She coughed thickly, hearing the wetness in her breathing, afraid to admit she was not improving. She reached for her glass of water, her heart sinking to see that it was empty, knowing she would have to fight her way to the kitchen to replenish it. She wasn't sure she could make it. And if she did, how would she get back to the couch?

The enraged crowd on the screen was pummeling the door to a lawmaker's office in unison. The door suddenly splintered, revealing a police officer hustling a politician away from the mob, a dog at his back.

She eased herself off the couch, moaning reflexively and feeling her fever literally rising as she did. "I can do this," she whispered to herself. With every step salty sweat droplets stung her eyes. "Maybe it would be easier to just let myself fall and never get up," she thought. There was beautiful release in the idea, but she fought it. Strange history was being made. The people were "rising." She was needed to witness it. Behind her on the screen she could hear the sounds of mayhem. The crowd had apparently spotted a target, the Vice-President, in the distance. Over the shouting she heard a plaintive calling a word that sounded like "mother." Then that voice was gone.

She'd made it to the kitchen; it wasn't too far to the sink. The yellow slim-line phone on the wall caught her eye. Where to go first? The faucet was dripping; it beckoned. She had her answer. She worked her way towards the sink, using the counter for support. The dripping seemed to merge with the percussive beating of her heart, and now the spinning of the room. The drip whispered, "Live. *Live*." She filled her glass clumsily and drank. She coughed up the first mouthful of water, spilling it on the floor. She kept drinking and refilling her glass, feeling somehow more courageous, if not stronger.

She just needed answers, she thought to herself. Answers would make everything better. It had to be better, it couldn't be worse than this. Maybe. Maybe she would be fine. Now the phone.

On the TV, an anchorman, shocked by the events at the Capitol, was asking a guest analyst for an explanation. Part of her tried fiercely to listen – but she had already picked up the receiver, and the dial tone drowned out the answer as she pressed 911 for an ambulance.

Fit in

Dela Muhundarajah

She shopped in her mother's closet
for something to fit into.
All she could find was a dress too big
or a skirt too long.
Nothing she wore satisfied
the bullies in her grade 7 class.

She stopped going to school,
after the lipstick was made fun of
and the powder was just too much.
On one of the days, it was pouring outside
and the girls in her grade 7 class
threw worms in her long, black hair.

Today, she tries harder to console her loneliness,
and avoid trying to fit in –
by wearing someone else's garments
and someone else's face.

The Bed

SHARON ROBERTS

Now 50, I have been living with mental health issues since my teenage years. Depression, anxiety, premenstrual dysphoria disorder, and postpartum depression turned into chronic depression and generalized anxiety. Treatments like medication, counseling, prayer, and family support, has helped me to go from non-functional to functioning. The unwavering support of my husband who had had a headache for nine straight months was priceless as he took care of our two young sons and his sick wife. However, when I am faced with stressful situations it often takes me back into those feelings of despair and hopelessness where I would often spend days in bed shut off from the world and its physical, mental, emotional, and spiritual demands. Chores and other responsibilities like house cleaning, grocery shopping and cooking fall to the wayside.

On this day, my husband who had stuck with me through thick and thin, losses and wins, advocated when needed and on occasion bleeded, came home tired after a hard day's work. When it was time for him to go to bed, he walked into the bedroom, looked around and said, "I'm sleeping downstairs. I'm tired and the room is a mess, the bed isn't made so I'm going to sleep downstairs. You know I can't stand it when the bed is unmade."

My nephew had spent the night and not only was the bed not made but his dirty diapers were on the bathroom floor, pillows were scattered everywhere and yes, the bed. *Really and truly, who do I think I am? This is not 'my' space, it's 'our' space and I had done it again.* The negative thoughts took over. For years, I'd done it, again and again. Not made the bed, leave books and clothes in the living room, kitchen, and the TV room, anywhere there was room. My nephew spending the night was no excuse and I had been at home all day.

I immediately felt bad. A flood of guilt and shame washed over me. I've made him upset, maybe disappointed, and surely frustrated. Possibly beyond frustration, and he had every right to be. Like a fired pistol, my mind automatically reverted to my default reaction. The negative thoughts ensued.

The tears welled up. *I'm a horrible person, how could I do this again, what's wrong with me and what am I going to do?* I apologized. As he headed for the stairs everything inside me screamed, *Ask him to stay*! *Tell him that I will clean up the room but he seemed to have made up his mind*. With tears flowing, I went into the messy bedroom and sat on the bed feeling sorry for myself.

After allowing the billowing of tears to flow for a few minutes, something deep within me stirred. A voice miraculously spoke. One that told me not to go there—not to go down that dark road that sucks me in like quicksand, causing me to feel worthless, hopeless, and helpless, whenever anything negative happens, whether it is my fault or not. The road that makes me isolate in my room for days overcome by defeat and depression. I listened to the voice that said *Don't go there. Just straighten up the room*. So, I wiped the tears away from my weary face and slowly picked up the pillows from the floor, threw the diapers into the garbage and straighten up the bed. Like a bent over bamboo tree that rises after a storm passes, My shoulders uncurled, and I thought *Wait a minute, Tonight I have the bed all to myself. I could spread my books out and read and write and choose to be in my happy place*. In my room, in our room, in my bed, in our bed. I was going to be OK even if it was just for tonight. It felt amazing to bounce back before all the air leaked out.

The Bridge and The Dam

Rana Khan

I had long thought that I was a bridge,
For people had been walking over me since I could remember,
And it felt only right,
Being at the service of others,
Taking people to their journeys
Being a part of their moving forward while I remained at a standstill,
Dependable, always there, taken for granted.

For I stood, day and night,
making sure there was no gaping hole in the pathways of those I loved,
And strangers too,
An all-weather terrain they could rely upon at all times.

However, the endless empty years have weathered me,
There are cracks in the asphalt,
Certain pieces have gotten loose, some have fallen in the abyss below.
And yet I stand, still magnificent,
all steel and iron, arches within arches, spanning the earth and skies,
But crumbling inside.

I have quietly watched the waters rise below me, through time and years,
and now they have bubbled up ferociously, raging,
The lakes are suddenly full, levees breached, estuaries overrun.

I'm trying to hold in the torrents,
But know it is but a matter of time
Before the waters submerge me, and those around me, completely.

I have got to find a way to dam my emotions somehow.
Only, I find that I have lost the language of dams,
Having been a bridge for far too long.

Courageous Decision

Lorri Bourgeois

On their usual Saturday visit to her paternal grandparents, Anne walked into a smell of fresh bread. Her grandma always made some sort of treat for her and her parents to enjoy while they visited. Anne took some fresh bread and a juice box, then went to sit on the balcony, like she usually did. This day was not like any other Saturday, it would change her life forever. Her parents stayed inside with her grandma, while she sat outside with her grandpa. She could remember everything from that day, as if it were yesterday, from the stormy weather to the comic book bathing suit and coverup that was a 9th birthday gift from her aunt and uncle. Grandpa leaned over and said, "let me see your new bathing suit." Of course, she didn't see any issue and was immensely proud of her new suit. He gently lifted her cover up and said, "such a cute bathing suit."

It didn't stop at that. He continued to touch her where no child should be touched. She felt scared. She pulled away so quickly she almost fell. She went inside and stood beside her mother, while asking several times to go home. The rain had stopped, it left big puddles which she would usually love to splash in, but not today. While crossing the street gripping her mothers' hand tightly, she told her mom, "Grandpa touched me." Her mother's face turned white as snow; her jaw dropped. "What do you mean, touched you?"

When they arrived home her mom carried her into the bathroom and asked her to show her where he touched her. She could feel her body trembling, but she showed her mom. Mom gave her a bath and told her that it was a good thing that she told, and that it was not okay for anyone to do that. Minutes later, Anne could hear loud voices echoing from her parents' bedroom, she didn't like when they fought as they did it many times. Her parents' marriage was not a happy one, they always fought over money or lack thereof. This argument was not like the others, it was louder and longer, with slamming doors that followed the screaming match.

Saturday visits stopped for a while. The events of that day stuck with Anne and soon she became withdrawn and afraid of the dark. She also was having nightmares and not sleeping in her bedroom for fear of somebody coming in and harming her again.

October that year, the visits to her grandparent's apartment began again. Anne was terribly upset as to why they would be going back to the place that gave her so many nightmares. Walking into the apartment, she instantly got a pain in her stomach and said, "Mommy, I want to go home." Her mommy assured her they wouldn't stay long, Anne was glued to her mom's side and refused to eat or drink anything. An hour seemed like an eternity. Did they not believe what she had told them months before? Anne felt as if she was to blame. Why didn't they protect her from the monster, why did they keep going back?

Things didn't get any better for the next couple of years, Anne sank deeper into her own little world where she protected herself, because nobody else would. Even though they continued to visit her grandparents, she found a way to somehow be alone in a room full of people. She fantasized about the freedom she would have someday. That someday came in the form of high school. High school would be the best couple of years, she would stay at friends' houses as much as she could. She also joined as many clubs and groups as she could, this would keep her at home time as little as possible.

Around the time of her seventeenth birthday, she met Mark. He was a good-looking boy who paid attention to her, even though she didn't understand why. Anne had gained some weight, she called it her suit of armor. The more she made herself unattractive the less anybody would want to touch her. Mark treated her like a princess, he made her feel loved; something she had never felt.

The first couple of months were amazing, he respected her and didn't pressure her for intimacy. One day they went for a drive, Mark told her he wanted to have a heart-to-heart conversation with her. She had it in her head that he was going to dump her. They drove to High Park, a spot they have been to so many times before. Mark began to tell her that he had never felt so close to anyone like he felt about her.

She was relieved but also so scared. He also told her he wanted to take their relationship to the next level. She explained she was not ready. "Don't you love me?" Mark replied, "I do love you, but I am not ready to make such a big decision." Shaking his head, he stated that if she did not have sex, then they were done. Anne couldn't understand why her prince had changed into a beast. She had flashbacks of her childhood. Anne very sternly told him "NO." She would not let anyone use her ever again. This infuriated him and he grabbed her by her hair and told her he wanted to show her how much he "loved her". The whole thing was over in minutes but seemed like forever. The stench of his cologne she once loved now smelled like rotting meat. She was silent as he drove her home. "I love you baby," he kept saying to her.

She got out of the car as fast as she possibly could. "I love you, baby," he yelled once more. She never looked back. She ran into her house and straight into her bedroom, where she sobbed for hours. Her mom asked her what was wrong, like she cared. Anne told her she and Mark had a big fight and it was over. "Oh well, it was bound to happen!" Right there she made the decision to not tell anyone. She was numb inside and sank even more into a deep depression, she stopped going out with friends and quit all the things she loved to do. If she didn't let anyone close to her, then nobody would ever have the chance to hurt her ever again.

Anne wasn't surprised by her mother's opinion. She always felt like she was "a mistake." Once she heard her mother say in response to someone asking why she did not have more children with Anne's father, to which she uttered, "I didn't want the one I had."

Tears streamed down her face. Why was she so unwanted? Anne went to a dark place, a place that she had visited so many times before.

Would anyone miss her if she wasn't there? Anne and her mother always had an exhausting relationship, sometimes Anne wanted to run away, but where would she go? Who could she trust with her innermost secrets?

Just before she turned twenty, Anne finished high school and took the first job she could find, waitressing. She also responded to a personal ad and was surprised when Johnathon responded. Soon they were spending many days together, finally someone who liked her for who she was. Christmas eve, he proposed, and she accepted. Something felt right. The happy couple soon started to make plans and decided to move in together.

The happy day arrived, hail the size of bowling balls fell from the sky, that didn't matter, it was their day to share with family and friends.

What a day it was, good food, good music, and the sense of a new day dawning. They honeymooned in the Poconos, far away from the reality of life.

Within months of the nuptials, the most wonderful news, a baby girl was on the way. They were elated. It was a hard pregnancy, Anne had some difficult times, but on August 28th, 1990, baby girl Symone was brought into the world. Anne vowed to her child, that she would protect her until the day she died, nobody would ever harm her or else they would have to deal with mama bear. Being a mom was the best thing to happen to Anne, she felt needed, and loved Symone with her whole heart.

Anne watched her mother crying with joy as she held Symone. Her mother smiled at her, and with that Anne understood. Although she could forgive, she would never forget.

Anne and Jonathon were so happy to see their little girl grow into a toddler and then a lovely young woman. Symone would do something that Anne could never imagine, she mended a broken family, not fully, but Anne was starting to let her guard down. After all she was an adult and now realizing that you can't grow by looking back. Anne and Jonathon faced some challenges along the way, affairs on both sides, and after ten years of marriage they split up for good. 2011 would be a hard year for her, Annes mother passed May 18th, after a long illness. So much loss, even though they had issues, she was still her mother and loved her with all her soul.

As Anne sits and reflects on the past trauma and all of the things she had to go through, she realized she wasn't alone, and bad things do happen to good people. She decides to make the courageous decision to write her story.

Strips of Light

Light in the darkness ventures towards the unknown.

Moses

FAITHLYN ALLEN

On a balmy summer's day, a baby boy weighing 8 pounds entered the world.
He had jet black curly hair, dark brown eyes, white flesh,
ten fingers, ten toes; they named him Moses.

He was loved, nurtured.
He had a soft heart and trusted too much.
He grew, went to college, got a job in the bank,
met a pretty redhead who stole his heart.

Money was tight so they chose to live on the rough side of town.
One autumn in the late evening they held hands
and dreamed of their future. He was just promoted to bank manager.
she just got a full-time gig as a nurse.

In the morning a realtor was coming by.
A man dressed in a colorful jacket, a carved cane, a purple hat,
women's shoes and painted red nails approached "I like your girl" he says.

They kept on walking, but he pursued; he grabbed her hand,
dragged her free, and pulled out a knife.
Moses, rushed at him, a struggle ensued,
she got the knife stabbed him in the heart.

Her hands are covered in blood.
She holds out her palms to Moses, shaking "I killed a man!"
He wipes the blood from her hand and tells her to run.
He will take the fall.

He ends up in a maximum-security prison,
cell block D.
He reads his Bible and talks to his cell mate about God.

A group of inmates poked by the devil
decide to teach church boy a lesson
They want to bend him over, penetrate him.
He fights and is rescued by a guard.

They hate him the more.
Two weeks later he enters the shower, they follow
A sharpened toothbrush handle,
razor blades on the other end

They make swift work; he did not stand a chance.
The stalls fill with red. He did not make a sound.
He slipped away silently looking steadfast to heaven.

Words, words, words

Habeeba

Sometimes
I can't,
find the right words.
the good

words
the generous ones.

when I say hi, I really mean
hello when I say bye
I mean don't go
just yet when I
say I missed you I mean
you were with me always. How can a
time come
when the words I say aren't for you?

I can't say this.
I can't say this.

Soul Search

DIANA SANDULESCU

On the journey to find my soul.
I realized this is a road I must travel all alone
For if I take you with me, we might end up lost
This road, I do not quite know
I can not be your guide
It will be like the blind leading the blind
You may wait here
Although I can not promise to return
I have to take this journey to find my soul
So that I can be whole

Faith in Action

CHRISTINA WALSH

I walk into the drop-in centre feeling frantic, overwhelmed and deeply sad.

Looking around to see which staff person is available, I feel more and more fed up. My heart is racing. Tears well up in my eyes. My eyes are burning. My breathing is shallow.

Faith approaches. I've known her for a long time. Relief starts washing over me. We had participated in peer-led groups about writing and art. I trust her and feel safe when we talk. Faith is a go-to person I actually have faith in.

"I notice you're feeling sad today. What can I do to help?" Faith's tone is soft. Gentle. Reassuring.

"Please, I need to talk in private. Do you have any time for me right now?" I can hear the desperation in my voice, but I don't care. I want help. I need help. Now.

"Sure, come into my office and we can talk. I've got an hour."

The breakdown is immediate. I start crying and awkwardly grab a Kleenex from Faith's desk. Words pour out of my mouth and soul. "I lost my dear friend Diane to cancer 16 weeks ago. She was my best friend for over 20 years. We shared many fun times together and tough times too. Some of my best memories include Diane.

And now my neighbour Brandy died – four weeks ago. She was welcoming. I appreciated her kindness and her dark sense of humour. Brandy did not allow difficulties to stand in her way. She was a happy, genuine woman, always lending a smile. And now I'm feeling more alone than ever before. I don't have many people I can reach out to or call or see."

Faith radiates kindness and moves closer to me. She says, "I'm so sorry. What a loss and not just one but two. I understand the struggle of losing loved ones. I didn't manage well when my boyfriend died from cancer last year.

I understand what it means to feel lonely and afraid, and misunderstood. Isolation and panic are not new to me, Christina."

Faith leans forward, taking my hand. My crying has stopped or at least slowed down. I take a sip of water and smile a little bit. "Faith, I trust you. The way you speak to me in a gentle tone. I like the way you take your time when speaking to me. And I appreciate you sharing some of your personal struggles with me. Thank you, Faith, for listening to me."

I pause, taking another sip of water. Faith doesn't let go of my hand, which makes me feel grounded and calm.

"Your pain reminds me of when I first got sober," Faith says. "Life felt like it was falling apart but really life was opening up. Getting better. I've been in recovery for many years now. I've had years of therapy too. None of us – you, me and everyone else – can do this kind of inner work without help. I'm doing this kind of peer work because I want to help people. I find it rewarding. Listening to brave people like you reminds me I'm not alone. And you help me get my mind off my own problems!"

Faith smiles. Then she lets go of my hand and stands up to stretch.

I share a bunch more stuff about my dear friend and lovely neighbour. I miss them and I feel angry that they're gone. They have been taken away from me. "Why can't more people be like them? Where do I meet new people and connect now? Faith, I don't trust many people. I value authentic, available people. I like being offered attentive listening. I prefer quality time. I like being with people who do not cut me off. I want to be with people who don't offer me unwanted advice or who belittle my struggles."

"I know it must be lonely for you and I appreciate how painful isolation has been in your life for such a long time. I am here to listen. I am here holding space for you. I am here to allow you time to ground yourself and allow you to speak from your heart."

Faith stops stretching and takes her seat again. She smiles over the rim of her glass at me.

"I have seen firsthand how you co-facilitate with so much love. You offer validation and time to others without interrupting them. I see you being a professional facilitator and making new friends. I see you attracting quality people into your life as you work so hard and diligently at improving your skills. Christina, I see you and I hear you."

I breathe in deeply. And I feel my exhale, long and refreshing. I sit up tall in my chair. I wipe my eyes. I apply Burt's Bees chapstick to my dry lips. "Thank you, Faith, for hearing me, for reiterating the good in me."

Our hour is up. Both of us stand to leave. I believe we're changed for the better. "Would you like a hug, Christina, before you head out this door and take on the world?"

"Yes, I would like that. My world needs more people like you, Faith."

Faith trembles in my arms for just a moment. When I look into her face, a single tear escapes her right eye. Taking my hand one last time, Faith smiles at me as she leads us toward the door.

"This world needs more people like *you*," Faith says gently. She steps forward and gives me one more life-affirming, faith-building hug.

Out of Hibernation

Vanessa Thompson

The sun rises, shining through the cracks of my bedroom blinds and kissing my cheek where I lay. I stay there awhile, listening as the birds sing me a new song. Slowly I remove the covers, one foot touches the ground, then the other. With all my strength I begin to make my way out of a long hibernation.

I get dressed, head downstairs and pour a cup of coffee before going outside to the porch. I go through these motions with an ease and familiarity as though it hasn't been months since I last emerged from my room.

The door opens with a creak, and I feel a breeze against my skin causing the hairs on my arms to stand up. Daffodils cover the lawn in vivid hues of pastel yellows, oranges, and pinks. They dance to a gentle wind and the subtle fragrance reaches me. This beauty emerges, bursting through the cold hard ground reminding me that something beautiful can come from my dark places too.

As I see the day laid out before me, I realize it no longer fills me with dread. I see endless possibilities instead. They gently invite me with open arms. It's no grand gesture but a quiet welcoming. I ready myself for this change, taking in the beauty surrounding me and filling with gratitude.

The Accident and the Incident

Roberta Taylor

Toby couldn't move any part of his body. His mind and heart raced as he tried to pull himself up. He felt pinned to the ground or the floor. There was a sweet sticky odor of fresh blood under his head. He willed himself to move but everything went blank, except he could hear the excited barking of Odo, Carl's dog. Toby wondered briefly where Carl was. Then he remembered and wished he had kept it forgotten. He knew for sure Carl was not Carl anymore. Odo kept barking and crying incessantly, angrily. Almost pleading for Carl to wake up. But they had wrapped Carl's Harley around a big, gnarled pine tree that had survived forest fires, lightning, and acts of God. Odo's pleas made Toby want to scream but then he wondered if he was also meant to go on to the next life.

There was silence as Odo stopped barking. Toby tried again to sit up. It was not his night. A huge bear was in the clearing near Carl's body and the mangled motorcycle. Then there was an incredible noise. Silence. Ambulances. Police cars. Somehow before he had died, Carl had called 911 and the GPS on his motorcycle had brought them into the woods. Toby might live. It was up to the bear. The bear stood up by Carl's body. Sniffed it and shuffled towards Toby who still seemed to be alive. The police sirens drew closer and Odo tried to keep the bear away from Carl's body and Toby. The sirens got closer, and Officer Allen Reed jumped out of the squad car. He looked around the dark forest, saw the bear, and pulled out his service revolver. He aimed it at the bear. The bear shuffled behind a tree. Odo kept the bear in his sight. Allen followed Odo through the forest. He felt afraid and angry at the same time.

Toby had passed out. He was going into and out of a catatonic state. He saw himself leaving his body. He knew he had a choice to live or die. He felt a calm presence all around him. For the first time in his memory, his entire being was enveloped by an incredible source of unconditional love. But that source pushed something back into his body. He felt and knew he was not ready to join Carl. But the pain he was in kept him in limbo. But while he was in limbo the bear left him alone. Then to his surprise he saw Carl. Carl was sitting on his motorcycle, not mangled. Smoking a cigarette, just being Carl.

He said to Toby, "You got to save Odo and that stupid cop."

"But how? I think I'm dead, Carl," Toby replied.

"Oh Toby, you are going to live another eighty years." And then Carl's particles slipped into light of all things and his soul ascended into the heavens.

Toby cried out, "Wait! I don't want to be alone!" But then another voice said, "You are never alone," and Toby slipped back into unconsciousness and pain.

Odo jumped at the bear when Allen tripped and dropped his gun in the forest. The bear knew, as did Odo, that Allen was vulnerable, exposed, and afraid. The paramedics had loaded Carl's body and Toby into the ambulance, not knowing the danger that Officer Allen Reed and Odo were in. They heard a loud scream as Allen tried to run away from the bear. Again, Odo started barking, snarling, almost angrily with the bear. The bear ignored the dog and started chasing Allen as he tried to get back to his car. He tried again, pulling in air with panicked rapid breaths. The bear stood over him, ready to strike when Odo found the courage to snarl and bite the bear's left ankle. Allen Reed fainted from the panic. But Odo knew he had the wrath of a creature five times his size. The bear turned towards Odo, claws stretched out, and ignored Officer Reed. Allen Reed, in a moment of clear madness, grabbed his taser, zapped the bear, grabbed Odo, and ran as fast as he could to his car, where he pulled the dog and himself in. The bear was shaking but he followed him. However, he did not catch up. Odo had found his new human in Allen Reed. Toby survived the accident, but the bear always had a profound shake after that.

Journey Home

JANET ANNE KENNEDY

I say the soothing words my family want to hear, telling them I will be with them soon and not to worry. I turn my cell phone off. I am tired of responding to the anxious text and voice messages asking where I am, urging me to get to the airport immediately. I have not met the "15-minute rule." As a Reservist, it was always strongly "recommended" that we show up for any job 15 minutes early. That way, even if someone was running late by a few minutes, they would still be where they needed to be before the deadline, ready to work with the team at the designated time.

At the main gate into the staging area, the email authorization on my tablet proves to be worthless. A ticket on the last transport leaving the planet to dock with one of twelve galaxy class starships is useless if said shuttle left forty minutes ago.

I know my two younger brothers, their loved ones and several dozen cousins are already aboard one of these vessels, being placed into a near death state, to sleep a dreamless sleep, waiting for the end of their journey to Proxima b., 4.2 light years from Earth. If all goes well, they will arrive at their new home in 6300 years. By this time, both Earth and I will be nothing more than a half-forgotten dream whispered through time.

I stand in the deepening quiet of my city, my neighbourhood, my home, my life scattered in piles around me. I do not need to travel thousands of years across space to find home; I am already here. Blocks of well-maintained brick and siding 3-bedroom townhouses built in the 1980's line a private road interspersed with mature oak, young red maple and unruly cedar trees. Rabbits and squirrels feast in the backyard gardens and play on the grassy common areas. The bike path behind my house meanders through both lush green open fields and areas of bush. I can watch the velvety night sky and feel the feeble attempts at star shine on my face rather than hurtle, unconscious, through the dark abyss between galaxies.

On Earth, time will be ephemeral. There is only one decade left, two at the most, before the sun fully transforms into its red giant phase, decimating those 3-4 planets closest to it. The intense waves of radiation will kill everything in its path long before the all-consuming firestorm. Death will be instantaneous.

I'm 54 years old and my life may well end before the sun's transformation is complete. I intend to enjoy Earth's soon-to-be extinct charms with whatever time is left to me.

To watch the vivid multi-colour sunsets, to hear waves lap against the riverbank, to smell wood smoke on the crisp autumn evenings, to taste raindrops on my tongue and to cuddle with my beloved dogs – this is what I define as crucial to my well-being. It is a comfort to me to think that I will most likely finish my life's journey by mixing my primordial elements with the rest of Earth's abandoned denizens in one final cataclysmic cosmic cocktail.

My family may notice a slightly dimming light in the sky where the sun once sat should they ever look this way from their new home.

No one will be here to witness the transformation of our sun from a red giant into a white dwarf star, or the charred planetary remains drifting aimlessly around it.

Silent Music

Manivillie Kanagasabapathy

memories whisper through my minds
discordant notes flowing into harmony
though fate pulls at my thread,
the vibrations ripple between us,
I know the melody of my absence
for it's found in the spaces between
each of your heartbeats.

Out of quicksand

MARIA HABANIKOVA

On the most romantic day of the year, I decided I had enough of romance and told him to leave.

Determined and brave, I let go of an abusive relationship. There was nothing in between and no turning back.

I sat face to face with a human predator at my parents' scuffed kitchen table. In the safety of my childhood home, I confronted a demon.

Little did he know, I rigged the game. I had been writing my way through the gunk of lies, deceit, and manipulations for days; I knew I was going to win.

His love was the overpowering kind. It intoxicated me into trusting without verifying and agreeing without thinking. From the very beginning, I was his perfect soul mate, the most amazing woman he had ever met. I believed him when he said we were going to be a team, start a business together, and live happily ever after. He planned and paid for a dream trip around the world. We never went.

He mirrored all my desires and gained my trust. He studied my weaknesses carefully; they were the strings, and I was the marionette.

***

As soon as he persuaded me to quit my job and move out of my own place, I was thrust into a bewildering cycle of good days and bad days. Happy times that resembled the start of the relationship alternated with hours of silent treatment to punish something I did or said wrong. He raised his voice more often, chastised and patronized me for no reason. He was a gifted orator; he convinced me that I was the problem in our relationship, feeling the wrong things at inopportune times, misunderstanding him and his 'toughness.' He was confusing me into submission.

I expected compassion and support from him when my grandmother passed away; instead, I was met with contempt and indifference. I never understood why my sadness or sensitivity sparked such anger in him.

He was gradually isolating me from anyone who might have tried to pull me out of the quicksand he wanted to trap me in.

***

Everything changed the moment a friend who suspected something was off sent me a few articles about the signs of emotional and verbal abuse. I realized this was the first time in months I was able to concentrate on reading. I was devouring every word as if my life depended on it and in fact, it did.

Empowered by what I learned and inspired by other people's experiences, I set out to explore my own.

I turned to my diary, my confidante, picked up a pen and bled. I felt feverish and nervous, riding a wave of sadness and rage. The reddened ink stood out on the blank page; I was no longer a woman erased. I was heading where he didn't want me, towards the truth.

I wrote about all the threats, reproaches, and empty promises. Suddenly, the unnoticed displays of his narcissism laid bare before me, tinsel of pretention and self-importance no longer able to cover up the sham.

With each word, I pushed away one grain of sand that had been suffocating me for months. Soon, I felt fresh air and saw strips of light. I re-emerged slowly.

With a relieving sigh, I dropped the pen and looked down one last time at the souvenir of a love that never was.

I got up smiling.

Victorious, I walked to the kitchen.

From Within Us We Become Us

Shannon Lintott

Tiny bud, Oh Sunshine dancer
Exploring the outermost edges
The tip of the universe
So new it is not yet green

Squinting eyes and pursed lips
We glare as our mouths turn dry
Grind our teeth and bite our tongues
Hands never relaxed

Yes, there is the desire, raw and immediate
To live again quickly
To remove the stains of difficulty
To recover and reinvent oneself

As fists move back to fingers
Colour is restored to our faces
We can see with wide eyes
From within us we become us

Roots to trunks and trunks to branches
Branches to twigs and twigs to buds
Old leaves leave and new ones arrive
A little further out, a little closer to the sun

Tiny bud, Oh resilient ones
Keep reaching and looking to tomorrow
You have already begun
You are the Spring

Looking to Grow

Themes of seeking a listener and having the empathetic ear of another..

The Attention Seeker

P.M. Jaye

I heard the man outside her door
talking
Not to worry, he reassured, she
was just looking for attention.

The bravest girl I ever knew
She climbed a range so high
there was no air
and rode a leopard fast and light
across the sands
all parched and fierce.

She trespassed
lands between here and there
cut into lines
refused to wear or do *anything*
that she was told.

And now her hair in waves
on linen white
My tender vine, my leaf.

I asked her why
She said I did not want to leave—
just lie a bit
and let the colours trail
and fly
kite and ribbon across the sky
sailing breath beneath.

She could not speak
her skin
a page on which she wrote
both scars and memory seared and bright
just looking for attention.

My Pen Leaks

Chris Kerr

Without fear
there is no courage

Jesus
Copernicus
Salman Rushdie

persecuted
for their words
of truth spoken,
of coercion levelled

the possibility
I could incite
thoughts
of retribution
excites me

Ingenious ideas
drip
from my pen

Surfer Silhouette

Irene Reilly

The golden maple leaves swirled around the emptied swimming pool outside as I stood sandwiched at the kitchen island between the oven and the overflowing living room. I marveled at Landy as she ducked and weaved from cupboard to stove, her pigtails flying.

"Nope, not quite ready," she announced as the oven door slammed shut, but not before a face full of steam escaped to herald the turkey roasting inside. Landy stopped momentarily as we all inhaled the aroma of roasting juices. Then she clicked back into gear; drinks were poured, and appetizers passed around. The Anderson family was a jubilant, boisterous, extended clan gathered for the Thanksgiving feast this afternoon.

This was Roger's *Ohana*. Landy practically adopted him when her daughter Lee brought him home to visit several years earlier. Roger eyed the pot of sticky rice steaming on the stove and beamed. He stole Landy's heart with his appetite for Chinese food and his easy smile. He loved Lee and fit into her family. Her Metis, Chinese and Scottish heritage aligned with his Chinese and Scottish. It was a match made in heaven.

Now he was in heaven, and I stood at the kitchen island in his place. The Andersons were a tight-knit family, and I was honoured to be their guest. Everyone was in motion—generations of family and extended family weaved and bobbed around, music played loud, and voices were louder so they could be heard over the din. Lee and her sister Jordan squeezed on either side of me like a big hug. We chatted, and their faces lit up.

"We're going to Hawaii," Lee said.

Her voice floated towards me; the words seemed suspended in the hot kitchen air.

"Hawaii?" I leaned in, pressing my hands to the counter to stop them from shaking.

"Yes, we'll be staying in Oahu and then we want go to the Big Island for a few days to see where Roger grew up." Roger and Lee had dreamed of going to the Big Island together one day.

"We could take Roger's ashes and lay them in the ocean," she said. (Lee had a small urn from Roger's memorial.)

The weight in her words, coupled with the sadness that swept over her face, broke open my broken heart. The noise and bustle of the kitchen evaporated from my ears.

"Are any of Roger's friends on the island?" Lee asked.

"Let me think. Who could show you around? It's a big island," I said.

Every fibre of me knew I should accompany these precious girls and escort my boy home. I could show them our house overlooking the Kohala coast, his old school, the places he played and worked. I knew the exact beach to lay his ashes. This was a trip I'd taken in my mind many times since Roger passed, but I hadn't had the strength yet to make it. A cold sweat trickled down my back.

"The turkey is ready." Landy's voice brought me back. Our conversation was shelved as dinner was served, complete with sticky rice.

"Aww, Roger, you should be here," I thought. I felt the joy he had expressed to me whenever he spoke about Lee's family. This was his Ohana.

Later that evening Lee drove me to the GO station in Oshawa. My heart was as heavy as the rain as we hugged goodbye.

"Thanks for coming," Lee said. Her long, black hair reflected the pool of light from the overhead parking lot lamps.

"I'll email you tomorrow with all the info on the Big Island," I reassured her. "Send me your dates. I'll get someone to show you around."

"Bye." Our voices were drowned out as the huge double decker train screeched into the station.

I walked towards the hulk emblazoned with tall green letters, GO.

"GO," I repeated as I climbed on board, choosing to sit upstairs in the almost vacant carriage. I leaned my forehead against the cold window, the platform below puddled in the misty light.

"I have to GO," I mouthed the words to no-one.

"But you can't afford it," replied the wee voice in my head.

"To hell with poverty," I argued with myself.

"What should I do Roger?" I prayed.

My resolve strengthened as the train gathered speed. "GO, GO, GO!" the grinding wheels screeched at me.

My eyes lost focus as they filled with tears. I felt a push, or was it a shove, as the train ground to a halt at the next station. I fell back in my seat.

"Call Jen," I thought, or was that Roger speaking to me?

I reached into my bag for my phone. I pressed the icon of her smiling face, fringed with blonde hair. The phone rang across the miles.

"Hi Irene, what's up?"

I heard Jen's sweet Minnesotan drawl. This was the same Jen who had invited us to the island when Roger was a baby, a vacation that had lasted seventeen years.

"Jen, I just left Landy's. The girls are going to Hawaii," I stuttered as the GO train revved up again. "I need to go with them. It's time to take Roger home."

"Yes," she said, like she was expecting my call. "I'll come with you."

Of course she would. To hell with poverty indeed, if ever there was a need to use my line of credit, it was now.

And so, it was three weeks later that Jen and I greeted Lee and Jordan with a refrain of "Aloha" as they arrived at Kona Airport. We adorned them with leis. Lee plucked a plumeria and placed it behind her ear with a big smile. Her beauty rivalled any of the island girls. We fell into a group hug as the dazzling sunlight dappled through the palm trees that fringed the Hawaiian Airlines terminal. We linked arms and walked to the waiting car.

The next day our toes felt the golden sand of Mauna Lani beach while the rhythm of soft waves kissed our feet. Roger's feet had first touched this beach in 1990 as a baby, barely two years old. He toddled, splashed, and grew to swim with the turtles on this Hawaiian shore. He learned to boogie board and catch waves. He was a free-spirited child fearless of jumping into the deep end. It was here on Mauna Lani that he attended preschool and kindergarten. His dad, Henry, and I worked at the luxury Orchid at Mauna Lani resort. This was the same beach where I went into labour with Brandon, Roger's brother, during the annual Turtle Release as Roger's pre-school class accompanied the procession of young honu turtles squirming to free themselves into the warm Pacific Ocean. The honu are a Hawaiian symbol of good luck in the form of a guardian spirit. It was Divine Providence that my boy's spirit should find release in these waters.

As a teenager, Roger's fearless nature fed on the adrenalin rush of edgy sports like skateboarding and surfing. He was more apt to drive his truck to the beach than to Kealakehe High School, especially when the surf was up. He dropped out of school in his final year. This prompted our return to Toronto. Roger didn't embrace the move at first but came eventually. By his twenties the illness of addiction had caged his spirit. He fought fiercely to overcome the demons. It was during one such two-year recovery period that he had met Lee as she walked her Cane Corso dog past the home he lived at in Oshawa. Roger, sitting on the porch steps, called out, "That's some dog you have there."

Lee smiled and brought Jax over for Roger to admire.

"He reminds me of the Hawaiian hunting dogs," Roger went on, his brown eyes smiled under his baseball cap. They chatted and walked together to the corner. The noble broker Jax brought them together. Before long, Roger was walking Lee home into the kitchen. That's Lee's story to tell, but I saw the love in his eyes at the mere mention of her name. Even with my love, her love and the support of all our Ohana, it wasn't enough. He relapsed, returning to Toronto for another stint in rehab and another desperate attempt to survive his addiction. The final blow came, a poisoned drug supply bought on a downtown street corner. He had laid his head to rest on the concrete parking lot. And now we who loved him would lay him to rest in his beloved Hawaiian waves.

We four broken-hearted women held our memories of Roger, and I held his ashes close to my heart in a small bronze urn. I set the flowers we'd picked that morning in the lush slopes of Pololu Valley into the kayak. The scent of plumeria and tuberose wafted on the warm ocean breeze. Jen and I waded into the turquoise water as we pushed the kayak off the beach. The girls paddled behind us. The sun shone above the snow-capped summit of Mauna Kea and bowed behind a wisp of a cloud. The palm trees saluted our regatta.

When we reached the calm waters beyond the reef break, Lee and Jordan pulled their paddle boards alongside our kayak. We held a moment of silence. Roger's life reeled through the cinema of my mind in technicolour.

"It's time," I said, gulping back my tears as twisted the lid of the small vase.

I leaned over and looked into the fathomless ocean and wondered if the honu turtles were waiting in the depth to escort my boy home.

A hand took the urn and shook his ashes into blue. Was it mine? I was out of my body, floating above the scene. We scattered a rainbow of Hawaiian flowers across the ocean surface. At that moment a swell broke across the bay. We were lifted as the wave barreled on towards Hapuna beach, the kind surfers dream of. I felt Roger's spirit catch that wave.

I exhaled and recited this Ode inspired by Elizabeth Fry's poem. The words had taken shape the night before as I sat on the lanai under the pitch-black Kohala sky perforated with a million stars.

"Do not weep.
I do not sleep.
I am the ocean breeze that blows across the surf at Mauna Lani where the honu play.
I am the diamond glint of moonlight on snow-capped Mauna Kea.

I am the sun on ripened papayas.
I am the mist rising from Akaka Falls
When you awaken in the morning's hush.
I am in the swift uplifting rush of the Pueo *in circled flight.*
I am the Northern star that shines in the Kohala sky at night.
Do not cry.
I am here with you always."

The wave curled on.

Roger caught the wave on Mauna Lani Bay, hanging ten in the big surf of heaven.

Lakeside

Mairon Bennett

I'm sitting in the red Muskoka chair
You're sitting in the yellow
And I'm trying
Trying
With eyes cast low and fingers laced
To tell you who I am
How I startle when someone shouts
Tossing their words in the air
How my phone rings and I just stare at it
As it inches across the table with each buzz
How I sit in the dark and wait for the light
Smacking bloody mosquitos away
How my dog's whims are my sins
Her darting fears, her manic mayhem
How I lose friends then never let them go
As their lives unfold without me
How I can recite a poem I wrote in Grade 4:
A shy weeping willow hides its dark and saddened face
Alone and so mysterious, in a cold and dampened place
A world so secret of its own
Whispering a willow sound
Its tears form a misty pool
The willow weeps, covering the ground
How an unripe tomato tastes like pumpkin to me
How fear feels like grit
How a lake wraps around me when the rain falls
How my mind shorts and fizzes
And you, in the yellow chair
With eyes wide open
As my stomach shifts and my eyes close
You say
Tell me more

Swimming Trilogy

KAREN JOAN WATSON

Grace Under Pressure – 1969

"Courage is grace under pressure" – Hemingway

[5 kids, on the side of a pool, anxiously huddled around Grace]

Her teeth chatter…

I didn't know. I don't know.

What happened, Grace?

He was there and I…I pushed…and…and…he wouldn't let go. I tapped three times. It's a drill. He's supposed to let go.

We just saw you spring out of the pool on the side. Like somebody threw you out.

You curled up. Are you okay?

I don't know. I snapped. I couldn't breathe.

We saw him hold you under. Something happened. You did something and he cried and went under.

You hurt him to get free!

Next thing we know, you popped up like a cork.

I've never seen you like that.

And he was limping when he pushed through the pool doors. He's a thug. Wild.

I was going to die.

Oh come on!

You were down there for a while.

Her teeth chatter, she's stunned at how close that was.

How close she was.

Later she thinks, I would have killed him.

That's a good thing to know. I can kill to save myself.

Saving Grace – 1977

[3 friends on shore surround Grace as she comes out of the lake]

What happened Grace? What happened to the guy in the middle of the lake?

It's okay, it's okay. He's a friend of neighbours across the lake. I've seen him out swimming before. He got a cramp. I was swimming close by, and he reached out for me like I was a lifebuoy.

Ho-ly!

What did you do?

You know I was a lifeguard. We train for handling people who are panicking. They can grab onto you. The panic makes them super-strong. They can crawl up and stand on you just to keep their head above water.

Really?

I never heard that!

We train over and over on what to do. It's a real thing.

Okay, well good.

So, what happened when the guy panicked?

He began thrashing around – too close. I didn't think, I just backstroked out of reach. I yelled, "HEY! I've got you. I'll tow you in."

But you were swimming away.

He slowed down his splashing to listen. "I'll pull you in with my bathing suit top," I said.

Oh, the guy must'a liked that!

Stop it, Annie, that's not funny.

Well, he listened. I said, "I'll pull you in. If you come at me, I'll let you go."

My god, did you really say that?

I had to say it twice. He nodded, so I undid my top and pitched the end toward him. He grabbed at it and started to climb as if it were a rope.

I would have screamed at that point.

I did yell: "No! I'll let go. Hold on and I'll pull you. Or I'll let go and that will be it. I'll leave you."

Did he calm down?

I could see him fighting himself. He was starting to get it. It was do or die.

Wait, would you have just left him?

That seems cold, Grace. You would have let him drown?

Would my drowning have saved him? It could have been the two of us going under. His only hope was to calm down.

But what if he just needed to hang on to you?

Annie, have you been listening at all? Jeez...

Sorry, sorry, I just can't believe it.

We just want to know what happened next.

He let go of the strap a bit. I got him to float on his back as I towed him over to his dock. I had to keep talking calmly.

Did he try to get you again?

Actually, he did. A couple of times he moved to roll over and I barked at him.

We got close to shore and he felt fine to swim on his own. I feel a bit tired now.

You used to do taekwon-do, eh? That's why you're cool, calm and collected.

You saved him.

She did!

God, Grace. You get into the weirdest situations.

I do, don't I?

Grace Full (Swimming, A Love Story) – 2021

Nowadays I trust my heart. I swim every day with my husband at Kingsmere Lake in Quebec, Canada, across and around the lake. Today the sky is blue, and the sun glitters on each wave. Brad hovers near shore, waiting for me to come in deeper than my knees. He's using a noodle to float; if I faint, he'll need it to tow me in. Five years ago, I had my first fainting spell; within months I had open-heart surgery to replace a faulty human valve with one from a cow. Someday I'll faint again and need a re-valve operation. Brad has never complained about playing lifeguard, or suggested I stop swimming long distances. He knows I can't.

I'm still only in up to my knees. I've been here for a minute, so it's time. If I go in too slowly, I'll stop when the water is below my navel, a visceral hard stop. In order to get in, I have to bypass that last step.

So in I go, arching and diving. The water is sharply cold for a count of maybe two, and then it folds around me like another skin; its temperature is mine. I just turned 65, but my stroke still feels smooth. I still turn and flip like a sea creature, a water baby, and glide in what for me is still a weightless heaven.

We swim like that, thirty yards or so from shore, and stop, treading water. And an amazing thing happens. A loon surfaces right beside me. She's sleek and dark. Her head pokes down to check out the fish below – a snack?

I actually coo to her. She turns her head to me, and stares for a moment – as if, I swear, to speak. Then she decides against it and slips under water. She's gone.

***

When I was five years old, I nearly drowned. I was swimming in this same lake with my 'twin' cousin, our first time together there after living an ocean apart for two years. We called ourselves twins because we were only a month apart in age – I was the older – and because of the bond between us. That day we were floating on an air mattress in shallow water, while our families suntanned on the beach close by. We started wrestling and laughing on the mattress, not noticing the waves pulling us out deeper. At one point my cousin rolled on top of me, and I pushed her off, and I fell off the mattress into the water, catching the edge with my fingers. The sandy bottom I expected to touch with my feet wasn't there, and I went under. I kicked at the water and half-pulled myself up by the edge of the mattress, getting my face clear, but as I took a breath another wave hit me and knocked me back down. I pulled out again, and one more wave hit me, and I went down again. Through the clear water above me I could hear my cousin laughing; she thought I was clowning around. The sound of her laughter didn't seem real, but my terror was. I was going down for the third time and had no voice, no breath, no hope. As deep as the fear was, my sadness seemed deeper. I couldn't believe this was happening. I thought, Is this all? Is this dying?

Then something pulled on my arm, a stronger arm, and slipped under my shoulders, and moved me up and out, into the light. I retched, and water gurgled from the back of my throat and out of my mouth. The arm laid me down on what I knew was sand. Adults surrounded me. This was not dying.

None of the grownups had noticed how far we'd managed to float in such a short time. It was my big cousin Megan who had glanced over and seen something wasn't right, and ran, and swam. It's a story I would remind her of more than once in the years to come, how she knew to swim toward me, how she saved me.

Leaving no room for trauma to set in, my mother immediately threw me back into the water with swimming lessons. Strangely, my greatest fear during lessons was holding my face *out* of the water and trying to breathe; panic took over then. Underwater, meanwhile, all was peaceful, and I could remember my strokes.

Maybe because of that quirk, when the time came, it took me three tries to pass intermediate swimming. I mastered the safety drill easily, but not the front crawl. With each failure, I begged to quit. But my parents didn't believe in quitting, not until we were competent. When I finally passed, my mother took out the rowboat and proposed an endurance test. If I could swim the length of our kilometre-long lake, with her rowing beside me, I would be allowed to swim with a buddy unsupervised. I started the swim feeling as unsure as I ever had. At the midpoint something clicked. The last half-kilometre seemed to take no time at all.

***

With the loon gone, I check back with Brad. He's good. The water is quiet. We swim together, and apart. I swim ahead and circle back. Then, alone, I swim over to a floating raft, anchored in deep water. I climb up the little ladder, and stand at the foot of a wooden runway, twenty feet long.

When I was in grade school, there was a popular TV show my family watched, called *Mannix*. Joe Mannix was a private investigator who took on dangerous cases and saved people. The opening credit sequence showed Joe Mannix racing full tilt down a long pier to escape a burning factory and diving straight out into the water like an arrow as the building exploded behind him.

On the lake we called it the "Mannix Dive." When my siblings were old enough, I taught it to them.

I take a breath, and now race myself over the raft in a running Mannix dive; it feels like flying as I launch myself straight out, splitting the lake's surface and gliding through the cool water.

I surface and turn on my back. The sun filters through my closed eyelids in pure ruby red. My face is out of the water – but I trust my heart and am not afraid.

The Trail Before Me

VANESSA THOMPSON

I walk alone with my thoughts. The trail stretches before me in a never-ending expanse of snow-covered forest. I slink into this welcome solitude as this space feels fully mine. With nobody around I can safely take off the mask I've been wearing.

I feel the tension release from every part of my body as it comes off. Time seems to stand still as I take in each moment breathing in the cool air and watching the vapour appear as I breathe out.

I look up and the clouds overhead take new shape as they peek between the tree branches swaying in the breeze. With each step forward I hear the snow crunch underneath the weight of my boots. Birds sing me lullabies reminding me that I can stay through this season too.

I gradually make my way to the lookout. I sit down on a worn wooden bench and allow the feelings I've tried to numb away break free. I let the tears fall down my cheeks that I've kept hidden inside for months. I sit there and observe the battle raging in my mind. I choose to continue fighting until this war is over.

I watch the sky go from blue to orange, pink, red then black. A chill runs through me as the winter sun begins to fade. As I get up to make my way to the end of the trail a thousand bright stars appear lighting my way. They shout to me that I don't need to walk alone.

Behind Every Weed Is a Beautiful Flower

Susan Purser

Life created with love
Life created by accident
Life created by horror
All lives created by seeds
Looking to grow
Waiting to be nurtured
Sprouting with hope and guidance
Wilting with pressure
Blossoming with the warmth of praise.
Guide your seedlings
Wrap them with sunshine
Encourage the ones that struggle
Behind every weed is a beautiful flower.

Watch and water that flower
See the rich colour of life explode
With memories past and present.
Each petal formed with
Memories of love
Memories of family
Memories of triumphs and tragedies.
All forming to create life
From that tiny seed
Not perfect
But blossoming and flourishing
Encouraged by rays of love
Not a weed but a beautiful flower

I Am From Words

Courage moves us beyond the self, into culture, ancestry, the cosmos, life as time, emergence, decline, a linear continuum, a circle. The story told and retold.

Frames From my Window

Maria Tereza Papaleo

Many years ago, my friend Maria Mascarello, who knew me very well, said that I looked at life through my window. Since then, this image has stayed with me. I have been thinking about this and have tried to understand what it has meant at different times of my life. I now realize that the limit of your view of the world does not matter because our views change. This is a human condition. New knowledge, new discoveries, and new environments should change our horizon.

However, it is not an isolated narrative. The frames through which we look at life are always placed in a specific time and space. Frames aren't an individual creation. Together humans build a meaning of life. Who we think we are, our identity, comes from the frames of our personal window.

As the frames are personal creations, everyone has their own stories to show this human condition. I choose to tell significant moments in three periods of my life, which will exemplify what it is to see life through our window frames.

I went back to the past looking at my childhood and youth. For sure my life was framed by my family's beliefs and lifestyle. The first support of this frame was given to me by my father. He was a strong and a good man, a good advisor for everybody around him. Justice and equality were the great values guiding his behavior and the way he educated his six children. However, despite this social recognition, he was afraid of women's power. For him, women could be everything they wanted, as long as they acted according to men's decisions. The world outside my window was supported by men's supremacy.

My mother gave me the second side of this frame. She was a beautiful woman, which everybody recognized. She had light. She attracted people who wanted to stay around her. Beauty was her place just as supremacy was men's place. She did not complain about men's domination. She believed that her beauty and men's power were both God's will, and that nobody can change it.

The third support was the idea of compassion and came from my two grandaunts, who were single women who lived with us, and both helped all our families. When I grew up, I looked at them with compassion, as people that had no voice in the society.

Finally, the fourth side of this frame came from my extended family. Fathers, mothers, children, aunts, uncles, nieces, nephews, grandaunts, friends were always welcome to my house. Children went to the same school; we vacationed together, and we had weekend lunches together. The importance of sharing life and respecting the collective stayed with me.

The next story shows my sight through my window when I married an executive. For almost 50 years I was an executive's wife. Coming from a middle-class family, I landed in the executive world. For many years, I was living as the wife in an executive men's world amongst other women. Like the others, I had money, comfort, and glamour in my life. But I wasn't allowed to be an individual person. In the same way that men were executives, women were executed. Executed because we were unknown; nobody knew about our lives or backgrounds. I was known and recognized only through my husband's position in the company. To support this lifestyle, I gave up my career, profession, jobs, and individual life. I had to forget formal or long-term jobs. Wives' jobs couldn't compromise the executive's mobility. My old identity got lost.

In this world, executives weren't in a comfortable position either. They couldn't share their personal lives or unveil their weak side. Fears had to be hidden. They had to always be strong and able to face challenges at their job and at home efficiently and successfully. They exchanged their family life for their career, self-realization, and public recognition. The executed women exchanged their self-identity for a lifestyle. Men and women had different roles to achieve power and to save jobs and maintain the lifestyle. Together they had to look happy and confident. Separately they made a huge effort to avoid exposing their real and personal lives. Happiness was framed by the company's success. Their lives were above the company's board decisions. At the end they are the workers team, they are not the owners. At least they are just employers.

The third story made totally new frames. It is a radical challenge to move from one's homeland. It doesn't matter where we go, the change will be total. I'm talking about becoming a citizen in another country when you are 63 years old. Why do people decide to leave their homeland to go to an unknown future? If you are young, society grants you permission to dream about a different life. When you are older you are supposed to be stable and avoid new experiences. You should be comfortable in your well-known environment. If you don't have a strong reason to leave, like war or persecution, your decision would likely be incomprehensible to many. Many would consider that following your children would be a dangerous choice. Parents became totally dependent on children, while elders they lost old and familiar references.

On February 28, 2019, I became a Canadian citizen. Ten years before, looking for new experiences in our lives, my husband and I had immigrated to Canada to live in Toronto. Both of us were retired and looking for new challenges. I had family in Toronto, two sons with families. I was close to them, but my goal was to be independent and to integrate by myself. Then my journey started. I had to embrace my new lifestyle and settle into a new culture. I must speak a new language and learn the social behaviors. I must make new friends and I should incorporate my old beliefs in the new life.

Now here I am, twelve years after my immigration. Well, different times mean different sights from my window. New knowledge, new discoveries, and new environments changed my horizon and who I am. But, to change and leave behind old toxic certitudes takes me a long time. I no longer feel guilty for seeing myself as equal or even better than men. I recognize that I am not a traitor to want to be beautiful or be myself amongst others.

I traveled around the world, went to beautiful places, and saw distinct cultures and people. I opened the door of the golden cage in which I had been living. For this I used every opportunity I had to change my view. I looked forward. Today I chose to paint my frame with the colors of justice, compassion, and respect to others in the values of my new country.

During my citizenship ceremony the judge made an inspiring speech focused on diversity, tolerance, donation, and acceptance. I realized that I made the right choice and I made frames with the hues of my past, my present and the futures possibilities.

I know I will deal with the limits of my window's frames forever. Getting out of one's comfort zone, achievements and knowledge are the tools to switch the window's frame. I realized the difference between *being* happy, *being* free and going beyond the limits.

Frames don't have the same meaning all our life. They are just the perspective that should make sense and be understandable for us. When we talk about seeing the world through the window, we aren't talking about truth. We are just talking about the meaning that the world has for us at that time. These possibilities were always there, but now I know that there are frames, and I can change them. It is up to me to use this wisdom to go forward.

Unrooting

Areeba Asghar

I have always imagined immigration as a movement of souls, an upheaval of identity, breathed out from the known to the unknown. It is the unrooting of tall trees, unplucking of their leaves and removal of the strong roots that had anchored them to their territories. How do we venture into the unknown? Do we stand in courage and bravery, or shrivel – shrivel like trees without the sun, burdened with weights of leaves we never imagined we would need to carry? Do we resist, resist to the slipping of life and identity and culture, or do we disappear, merge into the forest, a shadow of the ones we left behind?

I was a tree when we were unrooted, young but still aware, tendrils inching across land as we all learned to be. I was a tree, with colour, sandy browns and greens, vivid, now ordinary. But perhaps it's the forest, with its narrowing routes and winding paths that has molded us in its foreignness.

Replete

Ellise Ramos

A land of poison ivy tendrils, purple and dark blue,
creeping across my thighs, folds underneath my belly,
all over my back—
Like fingertips desperately reaching for the sky,
flesh that keeps stretching, breaks on the skin
to make way for the being inside of me.

Landmines of pus and volcanic acne
pepper my back,
once so smooth and silky
men gasped as I arched and purred
while they gripped my waist with desire—
now a wasteland of ruptured meat
tentacles of scar tissue
oozing and pulsating over my spine.

Thunder of pain persistent on my inner thighs,
a concave of chronic ache that carves its way into the night.
Every step becomes torture as I lug this alien body by,
trudging, heaving and dragging as Quasimodo
perches in between my shoulders and smiles.

This pregnancy has become a mind prison.
Free me from this heaving malady,
the claws of which keeps me
nailed halfway to the ground—
the parasite gnaws at my soul until I am kept silent,
letting days pass by in
dispassion—

Restlessly, tempestuously, agonizingly
waiting for the advent
of a newborn.

Cosmic Rebirth

MANIVILLIE KANAGASABAPATHY

When the world forgets you,
you are re-imagined.
Stardust free of constraints.

A new shape is yet to be formed
hope found though it has
not yet been lost.

Spaces between atoms –
infinite and minuscule.
A deep breath

a universal sigh.
The cosmic sound –
unending.

I Am Glad I Did It

Sharon Roberts

Sometimes it is difficult to face a situation, but it is important to have the conversation. Our past challenges can be hindrances leading to avoidance. However, recognizing what is more important in the present and the effects of life changes needs to be faced with one of courage.

She, my mother has endured a lot. One of her greatest challenges arose when her husband fathered a child with another woman. That of leaving her 4 children: ages 6, 5, 2, and 6 months old, behind to carve out a new life for herself and for them. She worked as a Nurse's Aide in her new country, a far cry from her nursing career which she had lovingly sacrificed to stay home and raise the children, as he had suggested.

Now at the age of 82 she's has been dealing with the challenges of the aging process. My brother got her a PSW. As a family we have always stuck together. My three brothers and I decided that the most important thing that she needs right now is to get outside, go for a walk and just move. Exercise for the aging body is as important as drinking enough water.

Yesterday she refused to go when Martha, the Personal Support Worker who suggested that they go for a walk after her shower. She implored Martha to just help her to go outside and sit on the bench beneath the shelter of the spruce tree out in front of the house.

I was angry, confused and extremely disappointed, but mostly confused. Should I talk to her about it or just let it go? No, my brothers and I had gone to too much trouble and it's heart-breaking to witness her health declining. So, I mustered up some courage and asked her why. "Why didn't you go for a walk with Martha yesterday?" With a look of resignation in her eyes, she replied, "Sharon, you don't understand. My body aches all over, night and day, when I move or don't move. I'm so tired. It takes everything I have to get up in the morning. I just want to sit. I also hate the fact that I'm losing my memory and that I have dementia. I know that exercise is good for me, good for my mind, but I just want to be left alone. I've worked hard to raised you and your brothers by myself for a good portion of your lives. I just want to stay in my little corner and do what little I can whenever I can, until the Lord is ready for me."

I could see it took courage for her to share her inner most feeling with me and yes it took courage for me to ask her and I'm so glad that I did. It revealed a part of her that I had never seen before and drew us closer together.

I am

Rooth Vimalanathan

I am from much more than one can hold
I am from a land of harsh terrain
And resilient people
from a broken land
And unhealed immigrants
A people
Holding onto what they can
Of their culture, their home, and their language
In a land that does not want them
In another land that was stolen
And on other lands that broke the rest of the world

I am from two worlds meshed into one
From the saltiness of a sandy, Serendipitous shore
and its inland's red ferric soil
To the polluted freshwater by Scarborough's tall bluffs
From savoury curries infused with spices and coconut milk
To greasy beef burgers and thick-cut home fries
From poverty
and rich experiences, both earned and from unasked for privilege

I am from my two first languages
Tamil by blood, English for sustenance
And from the others that fed my soul
From the romance of Europe to the respectful politeness
of the far East

I am from music and paints and doodles and numbers

But most of all,
I am from words
Whether those made flesh
Or dust particles mixed with the *Om* from the biggest bang in creation
Words seen, unseen, familiar, and not understood
I am the words of the universe
In all its diverse languages and infinite expressions

When the Time Comes

JOAN SUNDERLAND

As minute after minute passed, I sat staring ahead at the cracked concrete wall, my knuckles white from gripping the wheel. Reaching deep inside myself, I finally exited my car and headed toward the hospital entrance where I turned down the long corridor to Radiotherapy. Although I'd taken this passageway many times, I noticed for the first time the walls and floors were losing the battle to heavy foot and equipment traffic. Far too many medical carts, gurneys and wheelchairs lined each side of the corridor forcing me more than once to press up against a wall to dodge approaching traffic. Through the open doors of side rooms, I saw anxious patients awaiting their turns to be jabbed, x-rayed, or probed, all seemingly looking for ways to escape. The pervasive smell of chemicals I'd become so used to now assaulted my nostrils, and I struggled to hold down my breakfast. Initially stunned that hospital staff passed by me without a glance in my direction, it struck me that I'd also walked right by patients as if they didn't exist in what seemed like another lifetime but, in reality, was only a short time ago.

Reaching the clinic in the Red Bear Zone, I signed in and took a seat in the waiting area as far from the other patients as possible, as if this small act of rebellion would save me from being one of them. Picking up a magazine, I surreptitiously studied those around me. Most had come in pairs, leaning in toward each other whispering or holding hands. Some bore expressions of anxiety and bewilderment, signaling their futile struggle to understand how this had happened to them. Others wore faces devoid of expression; their eyes dull and unseeing, so consumed by the hopelessness sitting at the center of their being. I wondered how I looked to them. Did I also give off a vibe of despair at having to fight an enemy I could only temporarily keep at bay but never beat? I saw no obvious signs of illness, only the tiredness permeating every cell of their bodies as both the cancer and treatment sapped their strength. I noted I was the only one who'd come alone. What did that say about me—that I had no one who cared? Hearing my name called, I rose and followed the technician into the treatment room.

After I laid down, panic gripped me as she secured my head it to the table to immobilize it. Over the next unbearably long hour, I heard the interminable buzzing, clicking and whirring sounds of the CT scanner as it imaged my head. When it was over, I headed for the parking elevator in the Green Owl Zone. Struck by the absurdity of naming hospital areas in this way, I began to laugh hysterically only to succumb to wracking sobs. No clever artifice could ever disguise the fact that hospitals trade in pain, suffering and death. On reaching my car, it occurred to me that the disintegrating wall I was parked up against was an apt metaphor for my life.

I drove home on automatic pilot. As I walked in the door, I almost expected to find Dan working at his computer, music blaring. Instead, the empty house screamed silence. I slowly mounted thc stairs to the bedroom we had shared to rest and hopefully find respite in oblivion.

Five days a week for the next month, I had radiotherapy. At the end of the first week, a young woman I'd seen accompanying her husband to treatment introduced herself as Erin. After apologizing for maybe being too forward, she said she'd noticed I came alone and asked if there was anyone to keep me company. I curtly said, "No," but quickly added I didn't want to burden anyone any more than need be. The actual truth was, other than informing a few colleagues, I'd not told anyone, including my older sister Pam, for reasons I didn't fully understand.

"I know how you feel. It's a strain on families. Mark's doctor suggested we each attend a support group and we've found it helps. You should look into that."

Though irked at her unsolicited advice, I forced a smile and told her it wasn't something I was interested in. I was at once reminded of the many times I'd made this same suggestion to patients and feeling miffed when they rejected the idea, preferring to waste my time to discuss how they were feeling. I was relieved when Mark returned to the waiting room, and they left.

But this talk of a support network got me thinking about Pam. Though our relationship has been strained for several years, when I needed her most, she had rushed over to be with me. She had rocked me in her arms like she had when I was little, until I finally fell asleep, spent from all the crying and relating over and over again, the event that had changed my life.

I'd been catching up on paperwork while Dan was out jogging when the hospital called saying he'd sustained massive injuries in a hit-and-run. By the time I got there, he had died. I returned home in a state of disbelief and shock.

Standing alone in the foyer of the home we were renovating as I was finally pregnant, I begged God to take me too. My memory of the next few days is a blur; the only thing standing out is how Pam never left my side the day of the funeral as people came to offer their condolences. As tears welled in my eyes, I was jerked back to the present when I was summoned for treatment. After leaving the hospital, I called Pam telling her I wanted to meet up as I'd something important to tell her, feeling regret I'd kept her in the dark.

She came over the next day and before she'd even sat down, the words I'd kept bottled up flew out of my mouth like water bursting from a dam. I told her that shortly after Dan's funeral I started having excruciating headaches and numbness in my hands and although not overly worried told my doctor at my 12-week prenatal checkup. Pam stayed silent as I related how he'd called the day after my MRI saying he wanted to see me in his office that very afternoon. Vividly recollecting the chill that ran down my spine on hearing this, I was transported back in time.

On entering his office, I saw he'd been joined by an oncology colleague who wasted little time in informing me I had an inoperable brain stem glioma. My training told me I only had about 3-5 months to live without treatment and up to a year longer with radiotherapy. When the subject of treatment came up, I said I wasn't willing to risk my pregnancy just to ease my symptoms and extend my life. He soberly advised me to mull things over as there was no guarantee I'd live long enough to give birth. I left promising to call him with my decision by week's end.

During the next few despairing days, I went back and forth over my options. If I declined treatment, I could die before my baby was viable. But radiation could cause a miscarriage or fetal abnormalities and came with debilitating side effects. The day I was to call my doctor, I awoke feeling utterly hopeless and consumed with bitterness. What good was all my medical training now? I ran to the den and grabbed all of my framed diplomas off the wall and flung them to the floor, glass shattering everywhere. Mindless of the countless shards piercing my feet, I went to the bookcase and ripped page after page from my medical books before hurling them violently across the room, spines breaking as they hit the floor. Feeling pressure building up in my head, I tore at my scalp, hands coming away with clumps of hair caught between my fingers. I heard a woman keening like a wounded animal and I covered my ears to block out the horrifying sound. When I realized it was coming from me, I knew in that moment what I had to do. I went to the medicine cabinet and poured a near-full bottle of valium into my mouth and hurriedly downed the pills with water cupped in my hands. Just then, I felt a flutter in my belly and instantly regretted what I'd done. Bending over the toilet, I stuffed fingers down my throat, heaving everything into the bowl. After, I lay on the cold hard tile weeping knowing how close I'd been to ending it all. When I pulled myself together, I went in search of my phone to call my doctor.

After I'd finished talking, Pam wrapped me in her arms and we stayed like that for a long time, taking comfort from each other. When she left, I sat out back writing a letter to my unborn child. Sealing it in an envelope, I threw back my head letting the sunrays kiss my face while I breathed in the scent of the blossoming trees and listened to birds perched overhead. Though I'd often sat in this same spot overlooking the gently flowing river, I'd not been aware of how serene, yet full of life it was. I now saw squirrels scampering up trees, butterflies fluttering by in a kaleidoscope of colour and at the riverbank, a mother duck guiding her brood into the water. Amazed I'd been so blind to this, I gave myself up to the joy of sitting at peace among nature.

Arriving at my next radiotherapy appointment, I purposely sat beside Erin and asked how Mark was doing. I could see she was surprised given my rather cool response to her earlier attempt at conversation. She said he often felt very fatigued and nauseous and confided to me that what upset him most was knowing he'd possibly never be able to father a child.

"That's how he got diagnosed. I was having trouble getting pregnant so we both got checked out. We were devasted when we found out he had testicular cancer."

She then asked what I was being treated for. Her eyes widened in shock and her hand flew to her mouth when I told her I had an inoperable brain tumor and only a short time to live. I knew I'd been too forthright when she instantly jumped out of her chair and said a hasty goodbye when Mark returned to waiting room.

The next day, Erin at first pretended she hadn't seen me but then approached and apologized for having left so abruptly the day prior saying she didn't know what to say. Assuring her that her reaction was justified, I admitted the fault rested with me. I'd become so used to bluntly discussing a patient's prognosis, I often forgot the effect it could have on people.

"So, you're a doctor then. That must make it harder for you, knowing what's going to happen." I told her it was no more difficult for me than for anyone else and that accepting I'd limited time left had made me realize I needed to make the most of the remaining time I had.

From that day on, Erin and I grew closer in friendship. One evening she excitedly called to say Mark's PET scan showed his cancer was in remission and they'd decided to explore other options if they couldn't have kids of their own. When I didn't immediately respond, she asked, "Jen, are you still there?" Realizing I'd been lost in thought, I quickly said the news was great, but that she'd caught me at a bad time, and I'd call her back to set up a celebratory get-together. I really needed time to mull over the idea that had just formed in my head and also have a long-overdue heart-to-heart discussion with my sister over the child growing within me.

A few weeks later, it was settled. Mark and Erin would adopt my baby. We'd been to a lawyer who had drawn up the necessary paperwork for a private adoption. Pam had agreed at age 56 she didn't have the stamina to take on motherhood, but she would play a very active role in my child's life. From that time on, Erin accompanied me to all my pre-natal appointments and was with me when I learned I was having a girl who I named Lilly, after my mom.

Now as the weeks pass, I feel growing fatigue and although radiation has slowed the tumor's growth, my prognosis has not changed. On days when I'm not experiencing debilitating headaches, I sit out back writing in my journal which I hope Lilly will one day read. Pam often joins me and we either reminisce about old times or sit together in comfortable silence. Erin drops by regularly to help out anyway she can. She will be present when they induce me at 36 weeks and has arranged for time off work to assist me the first week. After that, if I need help, Pam is more than willing. I know at some point, I will no longer be able to care for Lilly and when that time comes, Erin and Mark will take her. While I wish I had more time to spend with her, I am at peace knowing she will be loved.

Warrior Queen

Diana Sandulescu

After a lifetime of trauma, a life full of losses
I look in the mirror and I try to understand
Who is this girl staring back at me?
She is whoever she chooses to be!
After all, I never thought she would make it past the age of eighteen

I look into her eyes and see pain and agony
That is not what stands out most
Much louder is the hope and strength I see
As she stares back at me
She chooses to be a warrior queen as she fights evil with kindness
Because everything that tried to break her is exactly what made her!

Memory is a Spider

Through courageous responses to the plights of deprivation and poverty, words create value, engender fresh significance, and establish meaning.

Apophasis

JL Allderdice

> "But sometimes in a man or a woman awareness takes place—not very often and always unexplainable. There are no words for it because there is no one ever to tell. This is a secret not kept a secret but locked in wordlessness. The craft or art of writing is the clumsy attempt to find symbols for wordlessness."
>
> – Steinbeck, "Journal of a Novel"

"Begin anywhere," they say. "Let the words flow."

Some say, "Write big; write the big ideas first."

Others: "Start with a detail. A loved one's eyelash, a mote of dust."

They say it doesn't matter where you begin, or how. Because what counts is not what you say, but what you leave out. Not saying—now that's saying. What you don't write, that's the key. Once you write everything else, look for what you haven't said. What you don't dare say. Dig into that. There lies treasure.

Not now, of course, but after. When you put the pen down. That's when the work gets done. Get some sleep or go for a walk. Think without words. That's how sense gets made. That's how discoveries are made. That's where magic happens.

Starting? Starting's the easy part. "Just begin; begin anywhere. You'll see."

***

Toby took their advice. He followed the writerly wisdom. He began. And he began again. He "just wrote," like they said, and soon he had whole manuscripts of "just writing."

It was what they said, it was easy! Soon Toby had books filled with his manic jottings. He had volume upon volume of raw stuff, the stuff that said nothing, ready for the "real work." Ready for the treasure hunt. The rewriting. The digging and polishing. The daring.

But you know, they don't just say "Start anywhere." They have some other sayings, too. Like: "Leave well enough alone." Like: "Some things are better left unsaid."

Sometimes they're right.

The Cost of Silence

FAITHLYN ALLEN

I remember reading a quote by Mariska Hargitay where she says "Healing takes time, and asking for help is a courageous step"

I cannot do it alone; I need help, but I am scared to show weakness

So, after working a twelve-hour shift, bones aching, eyes blood shot red, splitting migraine, I bend down hear the cracks and creaks as my body rebels, grab the frying pan and mixing bowl

Babe, "can I just make some eggs and toast?"

He grunts, stroll into the kitchen, slaps my ass and utters "how you gonna do me like that? I need French toast, eggs, bacon and home fries"

I smile and get to it, while he goes back to his game and scratching his ass

Babe, "how is the job hunt going?" I ask knowing

Man, these fools don't know good help. I went down to the employment agency, and they wanted me to be a janitor. You know I can't do that shit! I mean look at me

I think I am having a stroke. I scrub toilets all day three days a week and the other three days I wipe asses.

I cannot do this alone; my vision is blurred. My legs buckle, the grease splashes. No one comes to my aid, the frying pan flips, the oil lands on my chest. I lay on the floor trashing, mouth foaming. I cannot do this alone, I need help

In the distance I can hear him scream at the TV; his team has scored a goal

He turns his attention to me, "babe, what's up with breakfast?"

What will he do when he walks in on the scene?

What I could not say with words is so eloquently displayed by my twisted body

I cannot do this alone, I need help

Help me!

When I Say I Have Not Written in Three Years

Luxshie Vimaleswaran

When I say I have not written in three years
it is a confession
not a plea for help
please do not suggest that I just "write for myself"
this was not an act of celibacy
I did not choose for my anxiety to paralyze me
or my ability to digest whole parts of me
You tell me to just "write for myself"
And I feel the bile riding up my throat
Threatening to escape this prison
But there's something so seductive about darkness
that even when witnessing the brief effulgence of a glowing ember
It will remind you,
There are words still swimming in the murky waters of your stomach with no place to go
and that flame has long since burned out

you tell me to just "write for myself"
and I shut the blinds, pull out my journal, and pretend to write
and when I feel the words lodged in the back of my knuckles
I repeat
and I repeat
and I hope that muscle memory might remind me of what it is like
to have words function as poetry
to have blank spaces, breathe life in me
to have metaphors shooting out of my palm lines
because now, an empty page is the second most frightening thing for me to look at—
the first, old poems
a reminder of when I was able to string words together into garlands
when I could speak in flowers

when you tell me to just "write for myself"
I delete Instagram
in an attempt to delete the likes and comment section of my brain
delete the poems compiling on my feed
because how can I write for myself
when I'm an attention seeker
and I want to write like R.H Sin
and have millions repost the words I've written to their stories
with #facts #favorite poem
how can I write for myself when I want to write someone's favorite poem
how can I write for myself when it means unstitching every painful memory
how can I write for myself when my mother asks me to read to her my poems
And I delete the sex poems, and the ex poems, and I leave the ones about God
and finding myself
But she still doesn't understand and I think
how can I write poems that amma will understand

you tell me to just "write for myself"
and I try
on some days, I will sit by the moon and remember the way it used to lend
itself to me in the dark
The way its pools of light balancing on the flimsy pages of my journal was all
that I needed to feel seen

This is not a dry spell
It is a fertile period wasting away
By an intrusion of thoughts so powerful
that I'm afraid it might halt the very blood flooding my veins
But then I am reminded
That it has been this long, and I have refused to drown
That I have always kept my head above the water
despite the shackles growing heavier and heavier with each day

The land of eternal love

HABEEBA

in sheer innocence,
I'd wonder
at where love would hide.

much like Abraham
I would point to the
jewels
hanging from the sky,
asking Is this what I'm meant to love?

and when each would set and rise,
as such things do, I'd grow tired

lamenting that I would
be left
to wander
once again.

but now,
I see true love as a thing that doesn't hide.
as ever-present,
needing not
to be captured or
shrouded in petty disguise.

love is pure. Yes, love is pure.

simply because it originates
from the source
of all purity.

so may His love continue to reach us,
embrace us,

and carry us,
until we return
to the final home.
where rivers flow,

to the land
where eternal love lives

and where it grows
and grows
and grows

Dear Money

RENEE XU

Three (3) letters reflecting on the relationship between money and me.

I have wanted to write to Money for a long while. With more than 20 years of bumpy experience, I am strongly driven to reflect my relationship with it. I want Money to be my buddy. How am I going to gain the friendship? Maybe starting from a few letters?

#1 Dear Money,
I appreciate your existence. The convenience of daily shopping, business transitions and international trading is possible because of you. You have so many titles and variations, cash, credit, equity, debt, currency, capital, plastic, bitcoin, etc. Not sure how you would feel. It was so confusing to me, and maybe lots of other people.

What's the first time I was aware of you? No exact time frame. My parents, two assistant engineers, earned 56 Yuan per month in 1970s. 56 yuan is about $11 Canadian dollars. I am a bit startled by this number. $22 for a family. No, my father sent $4 to support his extended family every month. So only $18 left for four of us. No wonder I had no clue of personal finance for a long while. There was no surplus to sense anything other than scarcity.

No wonder
No wonder my parents are frugal
No wonder it was a moral
Awarding you a spiritual crown
The superstructure kept all
Civilians live with scarcity
No wonders
Just survival laborers

That's my humble start. Without being aware of the systemic issue, I was as cheerful as I could as a child. Somehow, my parents' conflicts regarding money reinforced a vague idea in my little head – it's a source causing troubles.

I would love to write to you more, to have a better understanding of our relationship, in the near future.

Yours sincerely
Hopey

#2 Dear Money,
I am writing to you again. I want to have you as my buddy, and I mean it. Every week I implement my investment plan, track my records, and reflect on my relationship with you. I have read tons of books about you. However, I used to be remote and still didn't know you enough to be your buddy. I'm more involved with my own emotions caused by you – greed and worries; hope and disappointment; Thankfully, I am not too scared. The first time when I learn that people committed suicide because of you, I was astonished and perplexed. To me, losing you would be unpleasant, but there is always a way to gain you back.

Then I realized I was too ignorant to the financial world. There is a concept called "leverage" which means you could amplify your money up to 400 times in the market. The super smart person who jumped off from a skyscraper failed the game; the money he owed to the market was around 10 million dollars or more. A consequence he could not face. A tremendous lesson about desire, risk and possible consequences.

When I deal with financial issues, I am a different person, using more of my brain; Even my face is a bit stiffened.

I need to stop now. Will write to you more next time.

Yours hopefully
Hopey

#3 Dear Money,

Today someone talked about reinventing oneself to live again. That is what I have been consistently doing. My real name means "reborn". I chose it by myself. Reborn in a new country, among different culture, I had to adjust, stretch, expand and eventually reconnect to the little internal me. My relationship with you is also a journey full of struggles. Starting with scarcity, broken connection and negative numbers of investment return: failure, failure, and failures again. I overestimated my capability of enduring loss and uncertainty. My sentimental reactions didn't help much. My imagination led to the frozen panic zone. What if the market kept going down? My guilt criticized that I wasted the accumulated amount of money through hard working. I used to have three to four jobs at the same time.

You were close and you became far fetching. I studied intensively, followed successful traders, read numerous classic books and more than 20 years of trials and errors. Eventually I figured out what's wrong, and what's missing: The origin of resilience. As a plant, without much roots, trying to grow fast and strong, inevitably, I was defeated by any storm, blast or drought. Sadly, no growth even in the best weather.

Being resilient is like leaves sprouting on a tree. The underlying force is from the root. To make the branch of personal finance stretch freely, it needs a strong life tree with established roots.

My efforts were spent on watering leaves, pulling trunk, or monitoring flowering buds, instead of taking care of the roots. In the past several years, I have been doing roots work, and that work wonders. Roots work involves self-care: allow, aware and accept myself. It also means to have the gut to face my imprinted life script, reconcile with the generational wounds, and start new lines on my spiritual space, resonating to innate self, to the universe. Through painstakingly practice, I am grounded with my values, learning style and family needs. And of course, be grateful. I gratitude all happenings in and out of my life.

I particularly appreciate your existence. The more I know about you, the calmer I am. You are there, like ocean water, flowing, waving, evaporating. What makes you ugly and greedy, what makes you glory and powerful, is human being's projection. You say nothing. Yet, you convey everything.

Yours appreciatively
Hopey

My Unfathomable Precious

Hasib Iftekhar

Have I had a supernatural experience? I sense trouble to even contemplate all the rummaging that's required to establish an answer.

In the depths of grotto where memories lie interwoven, one needs to dive-in first, uncover, then carry up the sequence of thoughts, before setting it out the cave. Very much the philosophical elevation one aspires to. Memory is a spider that weaves intricately—often just to trick its custodian. To reminisce on cue, is like dancing to the swindler's tune, involuntarily, take one off her crooked bat.

"Supernatural" is devoid of a scientific explanation, reasoning, or any laws of nature. That is, at best, what I had gathered from the sequence of intermittent hailstorms I call my prolonged life. It is reality bloated on steroids somehow to become magnanimously induced. To recognize a singularity as such, one first needs to acknowledge its presence: by being fully aware and then bear with it long-term. Only to become utterly perplexed in the process.

I am fearful of driving this close to the "recall" lane. Only a swerve, stronger only by a tick, might have me entirely consumed by the past and incapacitated to the call of the present. Crashed & Burned, simply.

Back to the opening question, and here's my "better-sweet" moment: I had once met a girl—and somehow the rendezvous became repetitive in mutual exuberance—and at one point in time and space, she said that she loves me.

Corny? Maybe. But ineffable to the point of my own bafflement? A hundred percent. Hands down, I would never understand the manifestation that prompted her mind that day, took her senses off guard and play it confused. She has been the most rational person in my realm of intimate knowing and yet, I remember how she was that day—in tears and totally removed from her calculated bearing. How her fingertips shook a little whilst resting on my face, I felt them there, reverberating. How her lips resonated, perhaps to her overbeating heart, and channeled a ripple of what had formed deep beneath—so fully, strongly, naturally.

I had no way: to mishear the words, misinterpret the declaration, and to misplace the notion.

***

Madness! to even comprehend—that I could finish talking about her,
To come full circle and then some, to cover all the corners and aspects, of her being.
And the history, O the history! The emotions, followed by them reactions, crimson.
Took my mind downtrodden—into a swirling slush-pool of sentiments—
Of which, she was the curator and conductor. I had never survived.
But surfaced later somehow, more mature, better.

Emotional capital, the harmonious sonata—
My baroness at dawn and Lolita at dusk.
She fills and then kills, with sparks that she hides
Between the blinks of those eyes, like distant searchlights.
Like a trumpeter she twines, and holds on
To me, heart-shaped long necks, and we flap, thrash and swim
In a conjugal float, staring at the sunset in each other's eyes.
I daydream of her laughs—like drowning into the
Sound of a misty fountain, and a sight of a stellar,
That is about to form a constellation.
My Bellatrix!
A sensual map I had drawn,
Like cartography veering off its course.
From the nape of her neck southbound, round and around,
To the Mons pubis– apex of an achievement.
How enraged and at peace I am, at the same time,
To the sway of her hips and the plush of her lips. I am
Pumped up in the vessels and steamed through the pistons—screaming at full vocabulary.
On to her mind, such jovial and kind.
From where on she unfurls, with a mix of stern practicality,
That hardly backs down or flinch—a sensational clarity of a clairvoyant,
A pragmatist by the by, and rational to the core.
She puts to the test all the (behavioral psychology) texts combined—
A fact she's blissfully unaware of.
She keeps to herself the lucidity and hence, I am forever bewildered.
Circling around my head still—the circumference of my limitations.

***

The greatest day unfolded not quite in its sunny glory but opposed to what goes commonly as romantic weather—the one with which, romcoms usually end. 'Twas the end of August and Autumn had already been venting around the corner. In an awkward attempt to harmonize, the grey sky blew down humidity and the heat veered intensely. Trees had already started to strip away—not with a sense of promiscuity but surrender. Around mid-day, the big city was bustling habitually, cacophonies everywhere and nothing in the vicinity, was particularly worth a promise.

We met, gracefully. I was on time to the cafe, to kiss my date with a warm caress. She looked gorgeous, illuminated in her all-white attire—an allure of poise in entirety. A soft embroidery on chiffon bejeweled the dress, to which, she had slipped on stupendously.

"Hey, I was thinking if we could talk for a minute and then order? You mind?" —she sounded unusually impulsive. I nodded whilst sitting myself down. She gets on with it with a vigorous ease. Paused at her emphatic points and cut all the redundant corners, she made the whole conversation: a lasting echo, seeped sweet in profundity.

"Last week was amazing, I really needed the time, off work, and all the schedules, to go away. Far. And I got back with so much that it all feels anew. So exuberant it makes me now; to see the photos, find the crumbs on my dress, and I keep reminisce on the time, the jokes, plays, all the slow touches.

On the hindsight, what it had really revealed for me was a set of realizations. Whilst musing over, I couldn't remember the last time I had re-lived an event in such a way. And then I started thinking about reasons inside one another, having thoughts chiming into tunes, they grew legs and scattered off in multiple fronts. Very loopy I know."

(She let out a jittery chuckle and assessed my grasp on things quickly and continued).

"And I had to dive in further 'coz it became too intense to take a moment. All the elements of the trip, except you, were familiar to me, in singles. Ordinary mundane bits they were. But the way they came together, gelled, and presented themselves, was in a whole new delight. It really was the best time I had, and I don't think I want to have it in any other way. I won't alternate it even by a tiny blink. Do you know what I mean?"

"I do"—my throbbing heart was beating up almost to a monotone.

Her eyes were held at me, sparkling the whole time. Now they became more eminent and started forming tears. My chest had banging bongos on, but I ignored it. The moment had me totally and utterly fixated on her. She sniffed there, a little audibly, let out a sigh and continued.

"Since the trip, I've realized something. Series of things in cohort that had me going. I tried to picture the whole thing without you in it and it seemed entirely different. Diametrically opposed to the one that I had 'with' you. You have been that one element—my magic umlaut, that fit in to the rhythm of the song and set its tone right, made the melody perfect."

(She breathed in slowly, but eyes didn't shy away from mine. She carried on.)

"Then I started thinking about the times we had before—since we've met. You were that special part of my life that I could hardly ever predict, plan on, or even comprehend a second before the congruous events had unfurled. We were alike in so many ways, in our thoughts, ideologies and mischiefs and yet, you kept on astonishing me, sweeping me off so naturally."

"And the times we had, mighty-petty crimes committed, and the hilarity between us, were implausible and I've treasured them all. So amazing really, were the seasons with you by my side. Cliché, I know, I'm hearing myself as well. But I won't dare putting it in any other way. I am being fully honest and probably the most I'll ever be. I can't help being helplessly sentimental circling around such introspections lately.

And I know how I feel. I know what I feel. And I let this be all consuming. I'm not resisting, because I see no point to it. It's not a fragile mindset that's episodic, it's not any form of misapprehension. I think I'm in love with you. Unusual might be the turning of events, or perfectly rational, but I figured that I had to say the words out loud, set them free from the pangs of my heart, right here, right now."

***

The kiss followed was warm and pulsating in the language of delight. Skin on skin in a nectarian indulgence. Humble to a newfound feeling, we tumbled down a hill like metaphorical haystacks—onto each other, twisting and turning, being abysmal to each other's postures.

I'm still caught in the moment, bouncing and spiraling of it surrealistically. My supernatural. See back then, I was "broke" by definition—a pauper with only an imagination to chew on. I had no hint of brilliance, motifs, or any disruptive ideas luminated above my balding crown. Nothing there to fancy onsite. And I was convinced to have carried on such a miserable dye.

But then of course, for a fugitive reason, she was meant to see things differently. I was not perceived as ordinary, but someone rather infused with porous wit and pronounced potentials. My perseverance was thought of as winning, guzzling forward in full throttle. My ideas and theories thereof, were conceived as scattered stars; awaiting a celestial marvel to align perfectly. And my profile and manners were all perhaps genteel and synchronized with mannish charm and elegance.

I still bemuse myself thinking. I throw darts blindfolded, metaphysically, hoping to hit that small circle of logic and reasoning. Maybe love is a natural phenomenon flocked-in through mystical prerequisites? Or maybe how Emily Dickinson had barely laid it: "Supernatural is natural disclosed." To me, it's still a game of guess.

***

Was it a scam of the hearts, or had she scratched a scheme out o 'mine?
I took my time, a decade and then some,
And then I turn in the bed, just to see
Her lips part still, reveals a grin—and happiness ensues from its radiance

Captured and Framed

Pursuing the inspired impulse or felt need to take up the pen, the echo of unkind words gives way to a more enduring kindness.

Uncertain Steps

Yasmin Newson

Can that key unlock my future? Will it unlock the doors between my present reality, help me cross the threshold into the future I'm striving to create? Will turning that key finally facilitate my transition into my unknown and uncertain futures? Do I really want it to?

What does it mean, that the key hangs suspended in a lock, without a human hand to turn it to unlock the door, or remove it from the door completely? It could mean the realization of my hopes and aspirations, if only I can muster the courage to turn the key, unlock the door, and step across the threshold.

Perhaps the key is a metaphor, of a next step, of an action I must take to transition from where I am now and on to what's next.

It makes me wonder about the obvious: what is a key? What is a lock? What are my keys? What are my locks? Not every key fits every lock. Not every lock is meant to be opened, nor should every lock be opened nor is every threshold meant to be crossed.

The key, perhaps, also represents unlocking and accessing wisdom that I am only dimly aware of and, perhaps, deny.

And then I think: some locks and some doors should just be left alone and remain unopened. Some other locks and doors should be opened and what lies beyond them should be explored.

There are many unopened locks and doors in my past. How do I figure out now what I should open and what I should just leave unexplored.

Not-So-Great Expectations

Jeff Cottrill

"The first time I read *Catcher in the Rye*," Dana recalled as she sat back in the pub booth and took another sip of her Pinot Noir, "I saw youth and insecurity in new ways – and also the hypocrisy of human nature. Even the language blew me away. The way Salinger made that kid come alive made me love books forever."

She closed her eyes and smiled as Nathan watched her. He chomped on a Buffalo wing as the overhead music switched from Lily Allen to Pink Floyd. She looked at him. He wasn't as dashing in real life as in his BestMatchPersonals.com pic but looks weren't everything.

"What about you?" she said.

"What about me?" he mumbled, wiping his mouth on his sleeve.

"What's a book that opened you and changed you for good?"

He swallowed. A long pause followed.

"Well?"

"*Redneck Jim's Big-Ass Book of Blonde Jokes, Volume Nine*," he finally answered. Dana assumed he was kidding, and she chuckled. But Nathan didn't laugh. He picked up another wing.

"No," said Dana. "I mean a *real* book."

"That's a real book. It's in my bathroom."

"No... not a joke book. I mean, like, a novel. *Catcher in the Rye* or *The Great Gatsby* or *Great Expectations*. Or maybe a poetry collection, or even a collection of David Sedaris essays."

Nathan thought about it for a few moments. Then he swallowed.

"Naw," he said. "I'm sticking with my answer."

Dana sighed and looked down at the table.

"Don't you appreciate real art, Nathan? I mean a *proper* book. Something more deep and meaningful than a dumb joke book."

Nathan put his wing back on the plate. He glared at her.

"Who are *you*," he said, "to tell me what a proper book is? How can you suggest I can't get the same kind of magic from my book as you do from yours?"

"I don't know how you can even compare the two." Dana was tempted to laugh, but it felt inappropriate. "*Catcher* is a classic, full of depth and honest emotion. It's resonated with readers for decades. Your book gives you a cheap laugh when you're on the toilet. Have you even read *Catcher*?"

"Of course I have. My Grade 11 English teacher forced me to. It's just some whiny, spoiled punk brat rambling on about how he hates everybody and everything."

"You're oversimplifying."

"Come on. Why would anybody read it these days, even if it *wasn't* boring?"

Dana ground her teeth. She wished she'd just stayed home and watched *Queen's Gambit.*

"And what's so special about your joke book, Nathan? Huh? Why pick a silly joke book over all the great works of literature?"

Nathan leaned back in his seat and squinted his eyes for a moment. Dana crossed her arms, hoping he was stumped, waiting to declare victory.

Then he spoke – in a low, controlled tone that blindsided her.

"When I was a kid," he said, "we didn't have much. No computer, no TV, no board games... just our tiny trailer with the necessities. Dad was always out of work and Mom was always bawling him out. My brothers were usually out goofing off, playing street hockey or whatever. I didn't have any real friends, so I was stuck at home, doing chores and listening to Mom and Dad fight. Nowhere to go, no one to turn to."

Dana stared at him.

"One day," Nathan went on, "I was outside watering the lawn when I heard this weird noise coming from next door. I saw our neighbour Skidface Sam – he was out on a lawn chair and laughing his ass off. Skidface Sam was the poorest, ugliest, filthiest guy in the trailer park, and he was always miserable and grouchy, and everybody avoided him. This was the first time I'd ever seen him laughing, and it scared the hell out of me. Before I could get away, he spotted me and waved the book he was reading: *Redneck Jim's Big-Ass Book of Blonde Jokes, Volume Three.*

"He let me read a few of the jokes, and soon, I was laughing harder than him. I'd never heard jokes like that before. The way Redneck Jim used such simple words to paint crazy pictures in my head... I'd never realized a book could do that. Skidface Sam let me borrow *Volume One*, and then *Two* and *Three* after that." Nathan paused. "The series only went up to three at that time, you know."

"You don't say."

"That was when I became Skidface's best friend, his *only* friend. We sort of had our own little book club. Soon, he stopped peeing in the trailer park's drinking fountain – well, for a while anyway. And from then on, I was addicted to Redneck Jim. Devoured every new volume of the blonde jokes, and also all five of *Redneck Jim's Sassy Smorgasbord of Polish Humour*. Those books really made those hard times easier. Anytime I was upset, or bored, or just wanted to pack it all in, all I needed was Redneck Jim to make everything better. Can you say that of your J.D. Salisbury?"

"Salinger."

"Who cares? The point is, Redneck Jim said so much more to me in his 'silly' joke books than your boring, whiny punk kid in *Catcher in the Rye*. Redneck Jim taught me that no matter how shitty life can get, you can still find reasons to laugh."

Dana couldn't think of anything to say.

"He also taught me," said Nathan, "that blondes are really, really stupid."

She blinked. Then she cleared her throat.

"Right," she said. "Well, my late mother was a blonde. And she had a Ph.D. in comparative literature. Wrote thirteen books. Won awards."

Nathan shrugged and went back to chomping on his now-cold chicken wing.

Dana stood up, put on her jacket, fetched a twenty-dollar bill from her purse and slapped it on the table. "I don't think this is going to work out," she said.

"Me neither."

"We're different."

"I guess we are." Without looking up from his plate, Nathan gave her a small wave using a greasy chicken bone.

She rolled her eyes and left.

It was early in the evening, although starting to get dark. Dana walked slowly down the avenue, peering into the shop windows, and feeling more depressed with every happy-looking couple she passed. Holding hands, stealing little pecks on each other's cheeks, or just sharing a mutual, peaceful silence...

A small, independent bookshop caught her eye, and she stepped inside. This was exactly the kind of urban indie bookshop she loved: cramped, messy, disorganized, nearly empty of customers and smelling like an old wooden house that hadn't been dusted in years. She started to look for the Classics section when she passed the humour one – and there it sat, like a trap set for her: *Redneck Jim's Knifty, Knutty Collectiokn of Knock Knock Jokes, Volume Seven.* She stared at the cover of the enormous tome, and a cartoon sketch of Redneck Jim stared back at her with brain-dead eyes and a shit-eating grin with a front tooth missing.

"Huh," Dana said aloud.

She picked up the book and flipped through the pages, opening to page 257 randomly. The first joke on the page read:

Knock knock.
Who's there?
Ura.
Ura who?
Ura stupid loser!! Ha ha!

Really, Nathan? This is your literary hero?

The next one:

Knock knock.
Who's there?
Cow.
Cow who?
No, YOU'RE the cow because you're so fat!! Ha ha!

Dana flipped to the end of the book. *Holy shit. There's actually six hundred and forty-seven pages of this?*

She flipped back to the page she'd been on. One more, she decided, and then she'd put the book back.

Knock knock.
Who's there?
Your mom, and I just boned her good!! Ha ha!

"Sorry, miss?" said a voice.

Dana's head jerked up to face the young man sitting behind the sales counter. "Huh?"

"I thought you said something."

"I didn't say anything."

"Actually," he added, "it sounded more like a laugh."

"I... I didn't laugh," she said, blushing. *Did I?*

She shook her head and turned back to the book. Last one, she told herself.

She read another joke. And another. And kept on reading.

Harried

Kristine Kaposy

Harried,
holler hail
aloud to the sound
as voice   the song
          lyrics sing
The rhythm sticks
The rhyme plays tricks

my favourite playground
right here   our online
'zoom-link-invite'
together   time

to begin
our session

search
for inspiration
prompts
where we start
to look
for what lies
underneath
the surface
scribbles

inscribed
on the page

Pry
Pray
Proclaim

Predict
Personify
Procrastinate
or with consonance
contradict

What else can paint
a picture so vivid
all at the same time?

Words, words, words...

Lost and Found

DIANA SANDULESCU

I had been lost for such a long time.
With every corner and every curb, I discovered nothing but darkness.
Terrified and desperate I remembered how I felt as a little girl.
The dark was my biggest fear so how did I even end up here?
As an adult, I dove right into it.
I did not know what to do or where to go.
I sat in that darkness.
Maybe someday someone was going to find me, but I was ready to give up.
I wanted to fade away.
As I began to close my eyes, I heard a small voice say.
Stay, please don't die today.
I woke up underneath a sky full of stars and ahead of me was a well-lit path.
I felt a surge of hope as I somehow knew this was the way home

Too much heart to stay

María Cristina Sabourin-Jovel (Queen María)

She knew she had to run far away from where she grew up to make it. That innocent-looking house in the well-kept residential neighborhood of Santos Suárez, just a few blocks from El Mónaco, kept too many secrets. Far enough from the downtown area of Havana to have a suburban atmosphere, where most knew each other and not many foreigners visited. Roses of all colors, cocotiers, and tall royal Palm trees, adorning each block. Numerous parks, four movie-theaters, ice-cream parlors, pizzerias, restaurants, all within walking distance, a real luxury to have back then and a great place to grow up in.

Three almost identical houses, standing next to each other, with a little garden in the front that seemed to welcome visitors with a smile. Hers, with so many varieties of banana trees, tropical flowers, and plants, green everywhere. The plátanos manzanos were her favorite ones. The little magical bananas, as she used to called them for their sweetness. Poppy red flowers everywhere, delicately covering the cement sidewalks, as they felt from the florecidos framboyanes, making the area feel a little enchanted.

Intricately designed white rejas in each window, adding even more charm to the façade of that two-bedroom house she grew up in, while offering protection. A large front porch designed to let the breeze move freely, the afternoon sun creating mysterious shades, she and her friends, used to play with, after school. Green walls with detailed white molding and high ceilings, pretending to belong to affluent families, not rich enough to live in El Vedado or Miramar. Floors with vibrant orange, blue, and red mosaic tiles, perfectly aligned, still shining today, more than eighty years after they were first installed. Cherished memories rush to her mind, overwhelming her. She cannot help but smile, seeing her younger self walking to school, holding her sister's hand. Both wearing perfectly ironed uniforms: red, white, and blue, just like the Cuban flag, proudly displaying those long black shinning tresses everyone used to admire them for.

Her father had a great job, which allowed the family to spend weekends in the best hotels of the city, the Habana Libre and the Habana Riviera, her favorite.

They visited high-end restaurants too often to think of it as anything special. Being the daughter of a foreigner living in a communist country, afforded her many privileges, she was often unaware of. Travelling abroad, shopping in stores without rationing, were some of those extras she grew up with.

She, the oldest daughter, had too much heart for her momma's liking. "Too naïve, too nice to make it in the world," she was told often. Wondering what was wrong with her, she tried to change herself, while begging for love inside that seemingly happy house. Listening to harsh criticisms became part of her normal life, being blamed for things she could not change. "You are too tall, your feet are too big, your lips are too full, your body is too developed for your age, you need to lose weight, your face is not as pretty as your sister's," some of the endless list of things that were seemingly wrong with her. A well-meaning attempt to make her tougher, preparing to deal with the harsh world she was to endure, as if making her perfect could compensate for the amount of melanin in her body and the racism she was going to have to deal with, later in life. Words, eroding her self-esteem, little by little every day, deep wounds deeper every time hanging upside down, far from the naked eye.

The one she loved the most in the world did not know how to love her back. She became someone else, hiding her emotions, eating up her pain, pretending to be OK, while knowing running far away was her only option. Dreaming about it too often to enjoy her childhood, she cried almost every night, thinking of herself as unlovable and ugly. Masquerading her tears with a smile, every chance she got, for no one was there to comfort her. Her father travelled too much for work. His kind words meant nothing to her at that time.

Her beautiful, seemingly happy, little sister, slept unaware of her thoughts, in the bedroom they both shared. Jumping to her rescue whenever she cried loudly, unable to tolerate anymore the excruciating pain, those long aluminum braces on her legs, inflicted every night for years. They were especially made for her, by one of the best orthopedic surgeons in Havana, her padrino, trained in Paris, where she was born about a bit more than a decade earlier. Cold ugly metal saved her from a complicated operation by breaking her skin and bones slowly in an effort to correct what nature failed at, just as her momma's painful words tried to make her tougher for the world.

She never dared to share any of her thoughts, for she was taught not to trust anyone but herself. Excelling at school was her way to make up for having too much of a heart and a body. Taking extra language classes in the evening, participating in every contest in school, dreaming about studying abroad as her only way out of that madhouse. Call her chicken if you wish, but she had no fighting chance if she had stayed. Her instincts were always right, even if she did not acknowledge them often.

The year of her freedom finally arrived. 1985, she was just 17 years old, fresh out of high school. She won the biggest prize of them all, a good girl's dream, her independence in a form of a fully paid scholarship, 9,909 km away. Ukraine welcomed her with open arms. A new chance at life. A new language she came to master and love, writing often about the sadness she was incapable to erase from her heart no matter how hard she tried. Six years in a foreign land, wishing she could be where she belonged.

The beginning of a life, separated from everyone she once knew and loved, far away from that charming house she grew up in, and from a country she still adores. She was sure she could not live without a heart. Unable to stay next to the ones who gave her life, constant criticisms sucking all the joy out of her, little by little every day, her dad's drinking forcing her to grow up too fast. Incapable of protecting her soul nor her sister's, she tried desperately to make everyone happy. Not succeeding, she had no choice but to save herself.

Words are still tormenting her today, their power finally diminishing each day. She is reclaiming her bareness, not allowing her mind to be pregnant with those unkind words anymore. A real battle she fights every day, claiming her new inner self, discovering slowly who she really is, letting go of the painful memories in that green house, forgiving herself for leaving behind everything and everyone she once loved, focusing for once on her kind heart and the courage it took to leave. She now knows she had no other choice for she had too much heart to stay.

See You Next Tuesday

Melissa Peters

Confining them to their tents for much of the day, the rain finally stopped. All that could be heard was the water lapping against the shore, the light rustling of the leaves and the crackling of the fire.

The scent of the wood burning was one of her favourites, evoking a lifetime of memories, and reminding her of loved ones lost, of days passed, and of times that could never be recreated. New memories had been made though, and they were worth every drop of rain, every single ache and pain.

She had thought before the trip, "I have *got* to use some of this time to write!"

The final night of camping, away from screens and distractions, had arrived too quickly. She had yet to pick up a pen to do anything other than play the "Find the Differences" kiddie game at the back of the Ontario Parks activity book.

She pulled her notebook from her dampened, sand-filled backpack and found two pens. "Not that one, the other one. The purple pen," she muttered, "because it matches the notebook and writes better."

She paused. "Stop stalling, Jackass!' she said louder this time, rolling her eyes, an exasperated smile touching her lips.

"What to write, what to write?" Shaking her head in frustration, she slammed little dots of ink onto the pages that mocked her with their emptiness.

And yet in the quiet, serene darkness, the words came easily for a page or two, but the plague of writer's block was never far behind.

She always fell back on writing letters. To friends, to family, to loved ones. The letters were never just letters. They let her put how she felt into words. The letters talked to people she trusted and loved without having to worry about how the words were heard or received. She was open and honest with the recipient and, more importantly, with herself.

After about an hour, she felt tapped out but revived. She realized that, even out here in the bush at a lonely campsite, the day of the week was the inspiration behind the sudden spark of creativity.

There was something comforting in the knowledge that her heart told her when it was time to write. That her heart felt the *need* to write. No clocks, no phones. Just Tuesday.

The Photo of What Is

Susan Purser

Walking the path of life
Among the many trails
Rivers, lakes, and oceans
Leaving footprints shallow on sandy shores
Quickly washed away.
Deep imprints fill with water
Sometimes stagnating
And then a wave crests – crashing down
Leaving pristine smooth banks
Overshadowing the memories of what was
And creating the slate of what can be
Reaching pinnacles along the way
Valleys, hills, and mountains
Lush with the warmth of success
Rolling through ups and downs,
Highs and lows.
Cresting the cliffs
Seeing memories in the horizon
Hazy on the good days
Bright with promise on others
Memories captured and framed
Filed away to be remembered
Creating the photo of what is.

Authors' Notes

I was lucky enough to be a participant in the group led by Lisa Richter. This experience was amazingly humbling and enriching. I learned so much about writing, poetry, workshopping pieces, and sharing one's heart with others. This is what writing is to me: the cleanest version of authenticity I ever shared with anyone. I am able to be myself without the fear of being judged or rejected. Many thanks to WCC, Lisa, and all my coparticipants for this amazing experience and for opening the world of creative writing to all. I hope it is not too ambitious to wish to be part of it again next year!

Queen María

The quality of the writing was high; I found the workshop challenging, so I had to bring my *A-Game*, but if you want to be a better player you have to play with better players.

Chris Kerr

I have felt privileged to be a part of the Write On! experience. I felt connected to my mentors/editors and fellow writers. I have received effective, constructive feedback as a part of my growth and development to continue improving and branching out as a writer. I feel empowered, heard, and recognized. This experience gave me lasting positive memories and more to come!

Christina Walsh

I began participating in WCC several months into this generation's global pandemic. Within a few sessions, unfamiliar vistas became available to explore, while new neural pathways began to be forged.

Prior to this, I had considered myself "just a math and science person"—the pursuit of creative writing had not readily occurred to me. So, the myriad benefits have been a welcome revelation.

David Gilkes

The WCC workshop was a safe and inspiring space to write and share. I was amazed by what we could create in minutes. The supportive and inviting environment helped me draw on emotions and experiences to create meaningful pieces.

Dela Muhundarajah

The Write On! journey has been such an amazing experience. Thank you to our mentor for facilitating a safe and comfortable space where we can learn more and develop our craft. It has been an honor to be part of this creative process.

Diana Sandulescu

I am so grateful to the collective for allowing me to get back in touch with the creative side of me. Because of WCC, I am able to connect with my community through the honesty and authenticity we share in our writing. Thank you, WCC, for allowing our experience to be a global and shared one, despite being in the middle of a pandemic.

Ellise Ramos

I will always be indebted to the Write On! workshop series. With everyone's support, I have grown more comfortable in my creative voice, and have the confidence to share my poems with others.

Habeeba

The workshop carried on with an intermingling of like-minded writers persuading self-expressions on paper. With open discussions, the process became alive and spurring with influence—thanks to the Moderator and of course, the Organizers. At a period of sickly sorrows, it positively blew in a breath of fresh air much yearned.

Hasib Iftekhar

The Write On! program nurtured courage in me to write the final chapter of my memoir Love, Grief and Hope. Writing in community with the mentorship of Anna, who guided our group through the ten-week program, our voices grew in community with weekly check-ins and encouragement. This program gave me so much hope in myself that I could do it, that we all could get to the finish line together. And we did.

Irene Reilly

Lisa Richter was my group leader. I was lucky to have such a talented poet as our group's mentor. She encouraged us to be authentic in our work and to take risks. My group members were supportive and willingly shared their experiences.

This experience made me realize that I had a community that understood and supported me. It also made me realize that for others to understand, my words had to be seen and heard by others, not just written down and locked away. My thoughts and feelings are validated whenever I write, there is no sense of shame or regret, just of a life lived as best as it can be.

Janet Anne Kennedy

The Writers Collective of Canada excels at building confidence in writers, no matter what level of experience. Participants are encouraged to express themselves freely in a supportive, non-judgemental setting, and I've definitely grown as a result.

Jeff Cottrill

Writers are solitary creatures, right? Not so fast! Working in community with other writers gets you to pay attention to what readers are hearing, instead of what you assumed you had said. Reading aloud to others brings caring feedback—and sometimes surprises—that will shape your rewriting in ways you may never manage alone. Thank you, Write-On! Thank you, Jay Teitel.

JL Allderdice

I learned invaluable tips on fiction writing from the WCC workshop, including building suspense, achieving a good balance between telling (narrative) and showing (scenes), and developing "consistent" characters. My writing has greatly improved as a result, and I feel more confident in my story telling ability going forward.

Joan Sunderland

WCC's Write-On! III was intense and satisfying. Each participant in our group wrote, listened and gave thoughtful feedback. Author Jay Teitel led our workshop and was funny, encouraging, inclusive. I stretched myself. It makes me proud to be part of this. Thank you, WCC.

Karen Joan Watson

I cherish the WCC and strongly believe that Pat Schneider's positive feedback approach creates a welcoming atmosphere that is encouraging and tremendously therapeutic.

Especially during these days of social isolation and uncertainty, due to the pandemic, my group workshop routine has helped me maintain a sense of community and creativity that continues to deepen. I have witnessed and experienced improved self-awareness, self-confidence, authentic revelations, creative writing and insights that are truly awe-inspiring.

Personally, the WCC has revealed to me the exceptional benefits of authentically sharing life insights with each and every participant! My creative voice and mental health outlook have been transformed from conventional critic to positive witness. Thank-you for everything you do!

Kristine Kaposy

With the fall nights closing in and a pandemic waiting at the window, we gathered around the Zoom hearth to warm our hands. Breathing with this rhythm of writing, reading aloud, and reflecting back to others, my head cleared, and my writing unfurled. Such a loss when it ended!

Mairon Bennett

Front Lines has introduced me to the most amazing community of mentors, writers and creatives! The energy and free expression, paired with the joy of creating and sharing, has made it a memorable experience that continues to feed my heart and soul.

Manivillie Kanagasabapathy

I am grateful to WCC's Write On! program for an opportunity to write candidly and courageously and to have my work published for the first time. WCC has given my craft a much-needed nudge along with a supportive community of fellow creative writers I continue to remain in touch with.

Maria Habanikova

Writing is the way that you express yourself without censorship. In the same way, you expose your ideas to diverse interpretations of your words. Writing with others in the Write On! program helped me try to do my best in writing. But it gave me more. To publish my work is to fly with unknown fellows around the world.

Maria Tereza Papaleo

Out in the real world of professional writing, one can become frustrated and disheartened with the constant edits, critique, and deadlines.

Write On! mentor, Shannon Leahy, showed us the ropes, pushing us to do our best, and to leave our comfort zones behind so we could be proud of the pieces we submitted.

The Write On! program is an incredible introduction into the real world of writing, combined with the love and support for which the WCC is so well-known.

Melissa Peters

I signed up for this WCC workshop hoping to gain courage, discipline, and critical feedback. I found all. I also found community. An invaluable creative experience.

P. M. Jaye

The Write On! program combines mentorship and writing in such a beautiful, productive way. I got helpful feedback from my peers and my mentor, and the sessions provided invaluable knowledge about the art of articulating thoughts on paper—and the skills of polishing them as best possible! Heartfelt thanks to all those involved with this truly wonderful program for aspiring writers in the community.

Rana Khan

Write On! lights me on, not fire, but something deep and tender, to the path of least resistance.

Renee Xu

The Write On! program is one of the best ways to encourage a group of people to get together and be creative. It has challenged me to be my best. I would like to see it continue into the future.

Roberta Taylor

The workshops were an amazing opportunity to simultaneously hone my craft while growing as an author in a supportive and creative community. The connection was so impactful that we still share our work with each other after the workshops have ended!

Rooth Vimalanathan

This workshop was a unique and incredibly supportive space that helped me to dive into my writing in new and profound ways. An appreciation for my voice and my story grew with each session. I am immensely grateful to everyone involved for giving me the opportunity to be a part of this extraordinary experience: for the courage, hope and resilience to continue writing.

Shannon Lintott

I was honoured to be part of this anthology. WWC has been a life changing experience for me as I now feel confident in expressing myself through my writing and then actual sharing it.

Susan Purser

The program was a welcoming environment that felt safe to share in. I learned a lot from the facilitator and others in the group. I'm glad I got the chance to participate.

Vanessa Thompson

The Writers Collective of Canada offered me a writerly home and so much more. It gave me a place to belong, to relax and play with words and forms, to discover my voice and express my thoughts in writing. In this welcoming home and supportive community, I developed the ability to craft my stories and the courage to share them.

Yasmin Newson

Mentors' Notes

In a world where a small group has always has the power to determine whose stories get visibility, initiatives like Write On! provide a safe and inclusive space for writers (from all walks of life) to share, experience, and create narratives that are often underserved in mainstream literary culture. I love the diversity of experiences that each writer has had the courage to share, and I love the warm and safe environment that the WCC provides. It's like sitting down at the dinner table with strangers who turn into friends all by listening, experiencing, seeing, and accepting each other's work just as it is.

Brittany Chung Campbell

"When in doubt, leave it out." This was a line that I applied to the way I lived my life. However, when presented the opportunity to be a mentor for the Write On! program, I was intentional in saying yes. It was the first time taking on this task and I didn't know what I was getting into, but I did it anyway and now my script is rewritten.

O. Stephen Peart

Gratitude to the WCC for taking me on as a Facilitator and Mentor. What a gift to mentor eight people emerging as professional writers on the CanLit scene. To say I was nervous that first session is to understate the obvious. But, after introductions and prompt-writing, we were all well on our way to becoming a community of writers.

It's given me opportunity to witness the growth and development of eight wonderful writers as they tried out some of the suggestions, and to expand my community of writers. I would happily do this again!

Bernadette Wagner

What an outstanding experience to work with this group of inspiring, generous writers! I arrived at each writing session excited and left amazed. Thank you, writers and Writers Collective of Canada!

Anna Lee-Popham

It was an incredible pleasure and a privilege to work with the talented, courageous, and dedicated writers in my group. I was inspired to witness how they pushed themselves creatively and emotionally, and the gorgeous, powerful writing that emerged as a result. Through their writing and their commitment to being their authentic selves, these writers gave me the gift of hope, courage, and resilience during these turbulent times.

Lisa Richter

The poems and stories compiled here are born of writers interacting. Through our writing, we feel, think, and say that which otherwise could not be felt, thought, or said; and just as our personal experiences warrant the effort that writing demands, you, the person reading this, are worthy of the care invested in these writings.

TG Hamilton

The Write On! mentorship was a wonderful experience—a nurturing and supportive community blossomed over the summer as we met and shared our words and thoughts. The diversity of our writers, and their unique stories, allowed us all to expand our view of the world and of others. I witnessed a growing confidence in each of the writers in my group, as each discovered and embraced their identity as a writer. I was uplifted and inspired by every one of them.

Nadja Lubiw-Hazard

After three years of mentoring in the Write On! program for the WCC, the most rewarding thing for me is a guilty secret: whatever insight I can impart to the members in my group, they end up imparting twice as much to me. They've been invariably interested, stimulating, lively, and committed. I just hope they don't feel cheated in the exchange.

Jay Teitel

The majority of us have had our inner artist wounded and silenced. Yet by writing alone and together we rebuild our courage, creativity, and confidence. I am a better human because of my time with these writers. I am a better writer because I listened.

Shannon Leahy

Authors' Biographies

Areeba Asghar is an undergraduate student who loves to write and has been a part of writing initiatives her whole life. She joined the WCC in 2021 and fell in love with the supportive and safe writing space and is awed by the powerful stories that emerge in the sessions.

Chris Kerr, after a career in nursing and social work was shortened by illness, attended film school. The camera held no sway. Writing and acting did. Screen writing led to his true love, poetry. His poetry has been published in *First Tuesday Poets Anthology, Front Lines: Bent, Not Broken,* and *Front Lines: Until The Words Run Pure.*

Christina Walsh is a long-time writer who has won several writing awards. Her work has appeared in Canadian writing anthologies and has been featured at spoken-word events and community fundraisers. Christina is a passionate believer in the power of voice, authentic connection, and trauma informed communication. She loves expressing herself through painting.

David Gilkes' personal journey traverses Ontario's rural and urban landscapes, and his writing displays a dramatic transition from elegant prose—reflecting the largely techno-scientific interests he pursued as a younger man—to more spiritual, introspective verses with strong cadences that currently preoccupy him.

Dela Muhundarajah is a writer based out of Scarborough, Ontario. She is a proud mother of two. Her poetry book, *Out of the Cocoon,* bravely reflects the emotional and mental impact of survivors of childhood sexual abuse.

Diana Sandulescu was born in Romania and faced challenges as a child and into her teenage years. From coming to a new country and learning a new language to overcoming traumas and addictions, she overcame those hardships through the lifeline of poetry. Her pieces are perfect examples of the themes of resilience and hope.

Ellise Ramos loves drowning in books, watches too many movies, and travels across Ontario to estate sales, hunting for vintage jewelry. Living with Bipolar Disorder I, PTSD, and ADHD, she is an advocate for mental health awareness and documents her struggles in her blog, elliseramos.com. Her other persona is a vintage jewelry hunter. You can see her collection at auctionhuntersdesigns.ca.

Faithlyn Allen believes that writing frees the soul and life from angst. Her work with those on the margins of society inspires her to write about topics and subjects often considered taboo. She is a certified Holistic Nutritionist and a Life Coach. She enjoys long nature walks, animals, and guiding others to live out their God-given potential and purpose.

Habeeba is a poet who enjoys contemplating love in all its forms, a perpetual student.

Hasib Iftekhar is a poet and short story writer in pursuit of his debut novel. Two sets of freelance fidgety fingers, laboring tirelessly to produce meaningful reads. City person, coffee lover and tends to talk 'beauty' or the lack of it around.

Irene Reilly is a non-fiction writer and a graduate of the University of Toronto's School of Continuing Studies Creative Writing Program. She is a member of, and volunteers as a facilitator for, the Writers Collective of Canada. She is currently writing her memoir: *Love Grief and Hope in the time of the Opioid Epidemic*. @RogersOhana

I am **Jacquie Irvine**. I am 58 years old, but I sometimes act like a kid. I love to write, been doing it all my life and will be doing it until I die. And I am full of unbound hopefulness.

Janet Anne Kennedy was born in Cornwall, Ontario, and now resides in Ottawa. Careers in the Federal Public Service and Canadian Forces Primary Reserve. Two diplomas and a degree, etc. Enjoys reading, writing, photography, genealogy, and crafts. Ongoing struggles with mental health issues. A beautiful work in progress.
https://www.facebook.com/janet.kennedy.3154

Jeff Cottrill is a fiction writer, journalist and performance poet based in Toronto. He has headlined spoken-word events throughout Canada, the United Kingdom, and the United States. Jeff has been published in several international anthologies, and his first novel, *Hate Story*, is coming soon from Dragonfly Publishing.

JL Allderdice has published in two previous *Front Lines* anthologies, and elsewhere over the years. His stories in the 2022 editions address Hope, Courage, and Resilience, but also (inevitably) Wordlessness: the ultimate and implacable failure of language. Special thanks to Jay Teitel and the Collective (Kathleen, Ahana, Hetty, Karen, and Marta) for listening.

Joan Sunderland is a former government policy analyst living half-time in Toronto and Winnipeg. Her retirement has enabled her to pursue her life-long dream of writing both fiction and non-fiction. An avid reader and movie watcher, she also enjoys spending time with family, travelling, and restoring old furniture.

Karen Joan Watson, BA, BFA, writer, visual artist, previously Government of Canada marketing manager. Hospice and housing volunteer, heart surgery survivor, parent, family genealogist, and caregiver to her elderly mother. Current projects: synthesizing life-and-death experiences and belonging. Defender of all that is lively. Lives with husband in Ottawa, Canada. kjwatson.ca

Kathleen Conibear was born in White Rock, B.C. and moved to Ottawa, Ontario at age seven. She has a B.A. with double concentration in Medieval Studies and English, B.A. Religion, and a college diploma in museums. She was short-listed by the Poetry Institute of Canada's open ages poetry contest in 2019.

Kristine Kaposy is a middle-aged mother with degrees from the University of Toronto, McGill, and a certificate in creative writing from Humber College. Epilepsy challenges her efforts to focus on a full-time writing career but, thanks to the WCC, she has published several poems, an essay in *The Bridge*, as well as initiating an elementary school creative writing publication at the Toronto Catholic District School Board.

My name is **Lorri Anne Bourgeois**. I am divorced and have a 31-year-old daughter. We live in Toronto: I have been writing for a number of years. This would be my first short story. We also have an 11-year-old Shih Tzu, her name is Lexi.

Luxshie Vimaleswaran is an experimental writer from Toronto, Ontario. As a second-generation immigrant, Luxshie strives to create a cultural context out of her racial individuality through her writing, exploring what it means to be an emerging artist in the Tamil diaspora. She uses writing in all forms to investigate parts of herself and her place in the multicultural heartland of Toronto.

A child living in the lithe body of a 45-year-old, **Mairon Bennett** loathes coffee, shrimp, and saying what she means. She is a future unremembered poet, someone with a broken brain whose sole career goal is to swim in lakes in the rain. Meryl Streep once called her "a decent actor."

Manivillie Kanagasabapathy is an internationally published, Toronto-based Tamil poet and writer who draws inspiration from her life, family, friends, and past experiences. Manivillie was one of the winners of the Toronto 150 6-word story contest and won both the Canada 150 poetry contest in Vancouver and the Scotia Love Books "stories in 140 characters" contest.

María Cristina Sabourin-Jovel (Queen María), B.Sc., M.Sc., M.A., is an Afro Cuban Canadian woman of mixed race who is passionate about social justice. She rediscovered her thirst for writing through WCC workshops after a 30-year hiatus. Writing has become an important part of her healing journey, and her unconditional lover during these difficult times of isolation. She loves easily and with a full heart, giving her all to what she believes in. Queen María now facilitates numerous writing workshops in conjunction with the Centretown Community Centre and Mood Disorders Ottawa. She was instrumental in setting up the first open BIPOC series of workshops at WCC, which she now cofacilitates with great enthusiasm and dedication. She is committed to fighting racism, fatphobia, and breaking stereotypes about mental illnesses and eating disorders, one writing piece, one workshop at a time.

Maria Habanikova is a Slovak-Canadian residing in Ottawa. She speaks five languages and works as a public servant and Zumba Fitness instructor. She is an avid reader and writer of creative nonfiction and short stories. She has been writing with WCC since November 2020 and became a WCC workshop facilitator in May 2021.

Maria Tereza Papaleo was born in Brazil in 1947. She was professor and has a master's degree in philosophy. In Brazil she worked in a volunteer capacity in adult education and in 1994 she co-founded a technology company. She immigrated to Canada in 2009. Today she lives in Toronto and proudly writes alongside fellow members of WCC.

As a kid, **Melissa Peters** would whine about being bored. Her mother's response was: "Go read a book!" Some kids complain when they want something. Melissa had to write a persuasive essay. "Words help explain me to others. And words explain me to *me*." Thanks for that, Mom! XO Melissa

P.M. Jaye is a freelance writer/researcher with a background in English literature and social policy. She lives in Ottawa. Her favourite words are: "Wait, I want to tell you a story."

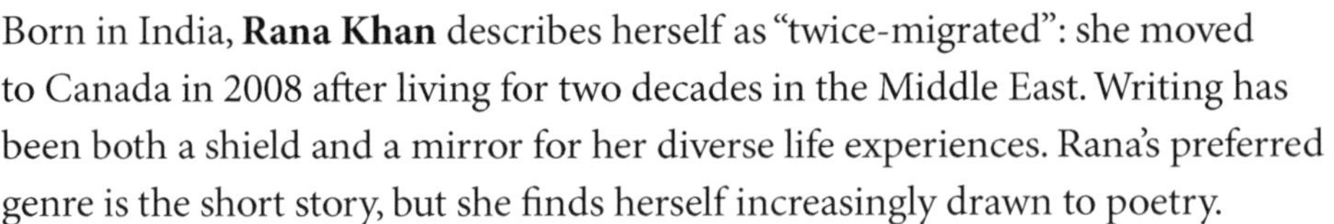

Born in India, **Rana Khan** describes herself as "twice-migrated": she moved to Canada in 2008 after living for two decades in the Middle East. Writing has been both a shield and a mirror for her diverse life experiences. Rana's preferred genre is the short story, but she finds herself increasingly drawn to poetry.

Renee Xu is a Social Work/Psychotherapist. Reading and writing have been her lifelong interests. She is working on her non-fiction book, *Dear Money*. Other than words, she also uses yarns as a media to express wonder: https://www.instagram.com/yarnwonders4u/

Roberta Taylor is an emerging Canadian writer and artist who has a strong interest in social justice and poverty issues as she struggles to maintain her independence, despite mobility and other health issues. Her first volume of poetry is almost complete, and she plans a children's book that she will illustrate. Roberta tries to do something creative and spontaneous every day.

Rooth Vimalanathan is an avid reader who draws inspiration from nature, personal and community struggles, and fantasy worlds. A lover of languages, stories, travel, and food, she aspires to invoke the senses and imagination through the dance of words. Rooth hopes to foster connection and bring representation through her work.

Shannon Lintott (she/they) began writing poetry on their mom's typewriter around the time they were learning how to tie shoelaces; they have been writing ever since. An avid nature explorer, world traveler, and journal scribbler, they are always creating something. Shannon is based in Toronto.

I was born in the land of many waters, Guyana, and moved to Canada in 1975. My name is **Sharon Roberts** and thanks to WCC, I was introduced to creative writing in Ottawa 2 years ago. It's been a pleasure and an education facilitating workshops for a mental health organization and a black organization.

Susan Purser lives on the beautiful Bruce Peninsula with her husband in a century-old farm home. Her winters are spent in the Dominican Republic. When she is not travelling or writing, many hours are spent making memories with her four sons, daughters-in-law, and nine grandchildren.

Vanessa Thompson is a stay-at-home mom who resides in Toronto, Ontario with her husband and two children. As a homeschooler, she values experiential learning and can often be found with her children exploring museums and nature trails within the city and beyond. It is through her love of nature, art, meditation, and family where she finds her greatest inspiration for writing.

Yasmin Newson is a Toronto-based essayist and poet. A graduate of the University of Toronto with an Honours B.A in Political Science, she explores the intersections of politics, race, and health through her writing. She loves to practice the art and science of fermentation and believes that creating is magic.

Mentors' Biographies

Anna Lee-Popham is a writer, poet, and editor. She is the co-host of the Emerging Writers Reading Series, an editor at *HELD Magazine*, and an MFA Candidate in Creative Writing at the University of Guelph. A recipient of the Janice Colbert Poetry Award, Anna's recent writing has been published in *Canthius*, *Riddle Fence*, and *Autostraddle*; shortlisted for the Fiddlehead Creative Nonfiction Contest; and received second prize for the *PRISM International* Pacific Spirit Poetry Prize.

Bernadette Wagner is an award-winning author and editor, poet and teacher, feminist, community builder, and influencer. Bernadette's recent work on uranium was shortlisted for the 2021 John V Hicks Long Manuscript Award for Poetry and the 2020 City of Regina Writing Award. In November 2021, she wrote 50-thousand words in 30 days for the National Novel Writing Month challenge. Before that, she launched the B Print Ink Writers' Room, a home for information about the writing and meditation webinars, workshops, and courses she offers.

Brittany Chung Campbell is a writer and book coach from Toronto. She helps marginalized writers go from just an idea to a compelling book with consistent sales and aims to create pipelines for lived experience (#ownvoices) stories to gain visibility. She works with authors as a sensitivity reader and facilitates creative writing and storytelling workshops while developing and facilitating corporate training programs about inclusive storytelling and diversity in publishing.

Jay Teitel is a Toronto-based writer and editor who's won over 25 National Magazine Awards in categories ranging from Sports to Fiction. He's written books, screenplays for movies and television, and stage plays, including a musical called *Alzheimer That Ends Heimer.* He is also co-inventor of the board game *Therapy*, which to date has sold almost 3 million copies world-wide.

Lisa Richter is a Toronto-based poet, writer, teacher and facilitator. She is the author of two books of poetry, *Closer to Where We Began* (Tightrope Books, 2017) and *Nautilus and Bone* (Frontenac House, 2020), winner of the Canadian Jewish Literary Award for Poetry, amongst other honours. She is passionate about building community and supporting emerging writers.

Nadja Lubiw-Hazard is a writer and veterinarian. She holds a Post Graduate Certificate in Creative Writing from the Humber School for Writers. She is author of the novel *The Nap-Away Motel,* and has numerous short stories published in literary magazines, including *ROOM, The New Quarterly, The Fiddlehead, The Dalhousie Review,* and more. A life-long animal lover and long-time vegan, Nadja's writing often explores themes related to the natural world. She currently facilitates workshops with the Writers Collective of Canada. Nadja lives in Toronto with her wife and their two daughters, an old black pug, and a feisty, fluffy kitten.

O. Stephen Peart (Jnr) helps aspiring writers find their voice through writing. He is the Creative Director of Released Expressions Media, host on the Xpression Podcast, and the author of several books, including *Released Expressions: the journey begins* and *The Last Write.* He is the father to two daughters who help him recognize the deeper meaning of parenting and life.

A professional chatterbox and story hunter, **Shannon Leahy**'s work has appeared in newspapers, magazines, and has been featured on radio and television. She's head honcho at Lighthouse Storytelling, a writing-and-speaking studio serving brave, beautiful writers. Shannon has presented storytelling techniques to school boards, funeral boards, health units, and nervous speakers wanting to influence VERY tough crowds. Her office manager is a cat intent on telling his life story.

Dr. Tom Gannon Hamilton: (BA Anthropology, MA Linguistics, PhD Education—sp. written composition/reader response) Established writer/author, literary theorist, instructor, editor, Tom is also a painter, screen actor, musician grounded in performance and dramaturgy. He has conducted workshops as an Ontario Arts Council Poet-in-the-Schools and taught writing in grade school, university, as well as community settings, enjoying success with inner city and culturally diverse learners. Founder/Curator/Host Urban Folk Art Salon (Partner – Toronto Public Library).

About the WCC

Writers Collective of Canada is a charitable organization that inspires exploratory writing in community to empower every voice, celebrate every story, and change the world.

Our unique writing workshop method ignites strong, authentic voices, targeting traditionally underserved populations and underheard individuals nationwide. We accomplish our work through trained volunteer facilitators and program partners.

Inspired by Pat Schneider, our workshops unlock innate creative genius, brave expression, and celebrate magnificent authentic voice.

Our special Write On! program, which results in the *Front Lines* anthologies, strives to amplify those voices through mentorship and publication.

For information, visit wcc-cec.org.

there is a quiet place

Kristine Kaposy

there is a quiet place
where all worry stops

the inner chatter
tangled in knots
of conflict   unknowing
               unfamiliar
contexts   Covid
               cannot touch

my Monday night
collective writing time
together   find

each   voice   remarkable
                    insight
unique
               creation

listen
to the truth
we are not alone

Manufactured by Amazon.ca
Bolton, ON